What's Mr. Hero?

"In the hero business you're either quick or you're dead," Sidney said in hushed tones. Daphne decided he was trying to scare them.

Suddenly five figures bolted into the front hall from the living room. They were dressed in black, like ninjas, but they were kid-size, no bigger than Daphne herself. She stared in surprise. Nothing like this ever happened in her old neighborhood.

One of the ninjas stepped forward and stuck out a hand. "You lose this time, Sidney," the ninja said. "Give me Mr. Hero."

Also by Mel Gilden

Star Trek®: Deep Space Nine™: The Pet

Available from MINSTREL BOOKS

by
Mel Gilden

Illustrated by
Debby Young

A GLC Book

PUBLISHED BY POCKET BOOKS
NEW YORK LONDON TORONTO SYDNEY TOKYO SINGAPORE

For Sidney Iwanter:
The Medici of Saturday Morning

This book is a work of fiction. Names, characters, places, and incidents are either products of the author's imagination or are used fictitiously. Any resemblance to actual events or locales or persons, living or dead, is entirely coincidental.

A MINSTREL PAPERBACK *ORIGINAL*

A Minstrel Book published by
POCKET BOOKS, a division of Simon & Schuster Inc.
1230 Avenue of the Americas, New York, NY 10020

Special thanks to Ruth Ashby.

Cover painting by Robert Brown
Illustrations by Debby Young
Typesetting by Jackson Typesetting Company
Developed by Mel Gilden for Byron Preiss and Daniel Weiss
Edited by Lisa Meltzer and John Betancourt

ISBN: 0-671-79898-7

First Minstrel Books printing August 1994

10 9 8 7 6 5 4 3 2 1

Printed in the U.S.A.

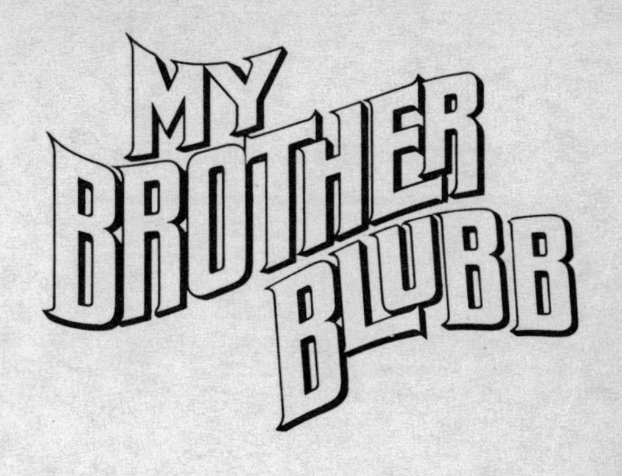
MY
BROTHER
BLUBB

ONE

Out on a Limb

Daphne Trusk peered out the car window at her new town and neighborhood and decided that it might not be too bogus. Actually, the new neighborhood looked a lot like the old one, with row upon row of neat lawns, and houses painted in fresh-fruit colors.

"This isn't so bad, is it?" Mr. Trusk asked as he drove along.

"No," Daphne admitted. The kids she saw looked more or less normal, which was okay as long as they weren't *too* normal. In her experience, a conventional kid was not very interesting.

"When I first saw our house," Mr. Trusk went on, "I noticed that the place next door was full of kids. You shouldn't have trouble finding somebody to play with."

Daphne wasn't worried about finding someone to play with. What she really wanted was a little brother—somebody she could help over the rough spots of life, somebody she could be a big sister to.

"What about you, Dad?" Daphne asked casually. "Any nice single ladies on our block for you?"

Her dad sighed. "Give it a rest, Daf," he said. "You can't hurry love."

"Mom died when I was a baby and I'm almost eleven," she said grumpily. "I wouldn't call that hurrying."

"I'll do the matchmaking around here, okay?" Mr. Trusk said.

They finally reached the new house, a big two-story job. The size made Daphne feel hopeful. Why would her dad purchase a house that big if he didn't intend to add on to the family? Of course, at the rate he was going, that could take years.

Next door was another two-story house. As promised, a crowd of kids, and cats, seemed to occupy it in about equal numbers. If Daphne couldn't find a friend among that bunch, she would be very lame indeed.

They parked and went into their new home. It seemed enormous because it was empty, and it smelled pleasantly of floor wax and fresh paint.

Daphne and her father spread out a picnic lunch on the living room floor. After they ate, Mr. Trusk showed Daphne around and let her choose a bedroom. She picked a second-floor room with two big closets and a bay window looking out on the backyard. The yard was green with grass and trees, but so overgrown it looked like a nature preserve.

The moving van arrived then, and they spent the rest of the afternoon directing the movers.

When Daphne went to bed that night, the darkness around her was lumpy and strange with full cardboard boxes. Still, the bed was her own, and it felt good to be in her new home.

Daphne listened to the house creak occasionally, and every few minutes a car passed on the street; but generally, nothing broke the silence. As if in a dream, she heard her father brush his teeth and turn off the light in his bathroom.

Daphne hated to pack, but she kind of liked unpacking. It reminded her of Christmas morning because despite the careful labeling, finding out what was inside each box could be a surprise. Also, unpacking in a new house gave her the opportunity to start over again, to make good on her promises to herself to keep her room neat and tidy. It had been a losing battle in the old house, but she was older now and might have better luck.

She unpacked for an hour, and then the beautiful morning drew her outside. Clutching the telescope she had unpacked from a box of dish towels, she went out to explore her new backyard.

Daphne trudged through the knee-high grass and weeds. In the far corner of the yard she found a weather-beaten plaster duck and three plaster ducklings. Near the ducks she found a perfect spider's web strung between two shrubs.

While Daphne explored, she listened to the shrieks and giggles of kids playing on the other side of the overgrown hedge. The kids sounded like fun, but they made her feel sad, too, because they reminded her more keenly that she didn't have a little brother.

Suddenly an idea struck her. Why not climb a tree at the edge of the yard and peek down on them?

It took Daphne only a few minutes to find the perfect tree and scramble up until she could see over the hedge with her telescope. The yard next door was a big rectangle of trampled yellow grass. A sorry-looking tree stood on one corner, with a tire dangling from it by a rope. Seven or eight little kids ran up and back playing tag, and cats of various sizes roamed everywhere. White saucers of cat food were scattered across the porch and yard, but Daphne didn't see even one cat actually eating.

Daphne zoomed in with her telescope on a

skinny boy about her age sitting on the back step. He wore a T-shirt and jeans, had freckles across his nose, and was reading a book. The fact that he was reading during the summer was a good sign. He might even be friend material. The type of book he was reading would tell her more.

Daphne adjusted her telescope but still couldn't make out the title. She shinnied farther out on the limb and looked again. *The Snarkout Boys and the Avocado of Death* by Daniel Pinkwater came into focus. Not a conventional book at all. Daphne was pleased. She had read it herself.

Without warning, the limb she was on cracked and fell into the next yard, taking Daphne along with it. She hit the ground with a thump.

Fortunately, the impact had been cushioned by the leaves and some smaller branches. All the little kids who'd been playing ran over. The boy who'd been reading ran over, too. "Are you all right?" he asked. She stretched her legs out in front of her. Her chin was skinned, but otherwise she seemed okay. No broken bones. A big gray cat sniffed at her shoes.

"I'm fine," Daphne said, catching her breath.

"Ask her why she's in our yard," one little boy piped up.

"What were you doing up there?" the older boy asked.

Daphne knew she was in trouble. She'd been caught spying, and now she was certainly trespassing. It occurred to her that she could make up a good story, but that was no way to start a friendship. "I just moved in next door," she said. "I wanted to see what the neighbors were like."

"Why's she in our yard?" the little boy still wanted to know.

"She fell," the older boy said.

"Why?" the little boy asked.

Daphne thought they could spend their lives telling the little boy *why*. "I'm Daphne Trusk," she said and put out her hand.

The older boy squirmed a little. He seemed uncertain whether he wanted to touch her. "I'm Harv Stuckly," he said. He looked around. "And these are my brothers and sisters."

"Why did she fall?" the little boy asked.

"Gravity," Harv said and rolled his eyes.

"What's gravity?" the little boy asked.

"I'm really sorry about dropping in like this," Daphne said. "I'll just take my tree limb and go."

"That's okay," Harv said.

By this time several kittens and kids were climbing around on the limb. It had quickly become a spaceship, a fire truck, a horse, a pirate galleon, and the world's biggest scratching post.

Thc little boy yanked on Harv's shirt. "What's gravity?"

"Susie, tell Oscar what gravity is," Harv said and pulled Daphne toward the driveway before either Susie or Oscar had time to protest.

"I'd give anything to have a little brother," Daphne said.

"You can have one of mine," Harv said. "I have plenty."

"Oscar's cute."

"Yeah, but he asks a lot of questions. Mom says he's going through a stage."

They moved to the front of the Stuckly house, and Harv timidly picked at the bark on the nearest tree while they spoke. Daphne already liked Harv, and he apparently liked her.

"So, you live next door, huh?" Harv asked.

"We just moved in yesterday. The telephone company transferred my dad."

"Your mom work?"

"She's dead," Daphne said.

Daphne's bald statement seemed to shock Harv. He swallowed and acted as if he didn't know what to say. Daphne felt bad about upsetting him. Not having a mother had been a fact of life for her for so long, it hardly bothered her.

"Do your parents work?" she asked.

"They run the store at the end of the block," Harv said. "You know, Buyer's Market?"

"I haven't been to the end of the block yet," Daphne said with a laugh. "Only to your yard."

Harv just nodded.

Under the tree was another white saucer filled with a pile of hard brown stuff that the flies seemed to like. Daphne pushed the saucer with her toe.

"Cat food," Harv said. "Meowser brand cat food."

"Looks gross," Daphne said.

"My dad bought a case of the stuff because it was on sale," Harv said. "He puts new servings out every few days, but not even the strays will eat it. They'd rather wait for the more expensive stuff he puts out when he starts to feel sorry for them."

Daphne barely heard Harv because she'd noticed something strange happening at her house. Somebody was climbing up an outside wall like a fly.

"Look at that," Daphne whispered to Harv.

TWO

The Tour

"Where?" Harv asked, peering around frantically.

"Up there on the side of my house."

"We should call the police," Harv said.

"By the time they get here, that guy could be gone with our stereo and our VCR!"

Daphne started running toward her house with Harv close behind. She had no idea what she was going to do when she got there, but she was too riled up to care.

As she got closer, Daphne realized that the guy was short and round—just some fat kid in a gray jumpsuit. He was climbing the outside of her house with the help of suction cups attached to his hands and feet. Each suction cup made a loud smacking sound when he pulled it away from the wall, then made it again when he slapped it on a little higher up.

"Hey," Daphne called. "What are you doing on my house?"

The kid stared down at them. Daphne realized he looked like Groucho Marx. He was wearing those silly glasses with a nose, mustache, and cigar attached.

"This is your house?" the kid asked. He sounded more apologetic than dangerous.

"You bet your life," Daphne said.

Laboriously the kid climbed back down the wall. He was briefly lost from sight behind some bushes, then he staggered out to where Daphne and Harv waited. He had twigs in his thick black hair, and dust covered the front of his wrinkled jumpsuit. On the lapel of his jumpsuit he wore a big yellow flower. Daphne was not an expert on flowers, but this one looked fake to her. All in all, the kid was really a mess.

"Sidney, is that you?" Harv asked with surprise.

"It's me," the strange kid said. He pulled off the Groucho glasses. Underneath, oddly enough, he still wore glasses. They were like the Groucho ones, but lacking the nose, mustache, and cigar.

"You know this kid?" Daphne asked.

"He used to live here," Harv said. "His name is Sidney Agenda."

"Hi," Sidney said and waved one chubby hand at her.

She stared at the hand suspiciously. It still

sported a suction cup. "What do you want in there?" she asked.

"Who wants to know?" Sidney asked. He glared at Daphne as if *she'd* been climbing on *his* house.

"It's her house now," Harv said.

Daphne didn't like Sidney Agenda's attitude. "You'll have to tell," she said, "if you don't want me to call the police."

"It's her house," Harv said again.

Sidney frowned and shook his head. "Hey," he said. "All right. I admit it. You got me cornered. I was trying to get the final project I made for my Methods of Crime Fighting class. Give it to me and you'll never see me again."

"The house was empty when we moved in," Daphne said.

"Maybe it's not as empty as you think," Sidney said. He wiggled his eyebrows at her, which, even without the Groucho glasses, was pretty ridiculous.

Still watching Sidney closely, Daphne pulled Harv aside. "This kid can't be for real," she said.

"He's a genius," Harv explained. "He was always doing experiments and stuff. Once he built a TV antenna that let us pick up *Star Trek* six times a day."

"Then why is he in summer school?" Daphne asked.

Harv said, "He's in private school. They have classes all year."

Daphne remained suspicious of a kid who would rather climb a wall than knock on a front door. She almost told him to take his lumps in his class. What did he say it was? Methods of Crime Fighting? The name sounded made up.

But a final project was serious. She had lost an important assignment down a storm drain during some bad weather in her old neighborhood. She'd been convinced she'd spend the rest of her life in the fourth grade until her teacher gave her another week to spell out the preamble to the U.S. Constitution in alphabet macaroni.

Besides, following Sidney while he hunted through her house might be real educational.

"All right," she said.

"Hey," Sidney said and gave her a thumbs-up sign. If Daphne hadn't known he was a genius, she would have been sure he was goofy.

She led Sidney and Harv inside. Sidney gave disapproving glances at the cardboard boxes, but Daphne didn't care what he thought.

"At my old school," Daphne said, "we didn't have a class like Methods of Crime-fighting."

"We have special courses. You wouldn't understand," Sidney said as he strode across the living room to the far wall. He tapped twice on the wall.

"Try me," Daphne said coldly as the wall swung open to reveal a long metal panel. But when she saw the colorful arrangement of blinking lights, gauges, and switches, she forgot her anger.

Harv did not seem astonished. "What's that?" he asked matter-of-factly.

"Time machine junction box," Sidney said.

Apparently, Daphne decided, he thought they were stupid. "You don't have to be a genius to know time machines are just in books," she said.

"Oh, yeah, I forgot," Sidney said sarcastically. He swung the wall closed.

"Whatever it is," Daphne said, a little exasperated, "I hope it's not dangerous. I have to live here."

"And I'm next door," Harv said.

"You've got nothing to worry about. Me and my aunt Millicent lived here for years and nothing happened."

Sidney turned and wandered through the house, stopping now and then to peek behind a hidden door. The house had secret passageways, secret rooms, and secret equipment everywhere.

Daphne thought about telling her father, but then decided he might say they should move out. Though not totally satisfied that the house was as safe as Sidney said it was, Daphne did not want to give up the chance to explore it more. It was too amazing to take in all at once.

Beneath the trapdoor in the family room lay a stone stairway that led into darkness. A garbagy smell rose up from it along with the lapping of water.

"What's down there?" Daphne asked.

"The River Thames," Sidney said as he let the trap fall with a bang.

"That's impossible," Harv said. "The Thames flows through London in England. That's thousands of miles from here."

Sidney silently studied Harv for a moment. "Hey," he finally said, "you two are full of useful information. Maybe you should open a school yourselves."

Daphne was completely confused. One minute Sidney talked like a genius, and the next he acted nuts. Plus he kept treating them as if *they* were the idiots, which really rubbed Daphne the wrong way.

From behind the wall at the back of the upstairs linen closet he pulled out a spherical dark metal object, about the size of a basketball. Colored buttons flashed on it, and three long transparent rods were rammed through it. It made tiny electronic bleeps, as if it were laughing to itself. Delighted, Sidney turned it over in his hands.

"Class project?" Harv asked.

"Nope," Sidney said. "It's kind of a radio. It calls things."

"Calls what?" Daphne asked. "Enemy submarines? Taxicabs? Dogs? Flying saucers? Buses?"

"Yeah," Sidney said, agreeing to all of Daphne's suggestions.

His easy answer made Daphne angrier than if he'd said nothing. She wouldn't mind him keeping secrets. Everybody had them. What she minded was his stuck-up snotty manner.

"Get out of my house," Daphne said to Sidney. Sidney marched away without a backward glance.

Harv touched her arm. "He takes a little getting used to."

"I don't think I want to bother," Daphne said. She followed Sidney along the upstairs hallway and was shocked when instead of going down the stairs, he went into her room. She hurried in after him.

Sidney lifted the seat under the bay window, revealing a space big enough to hide a dead body, should that ever become necessary. From it, he lifted out a large glass jar filled with purple stuff and held it up proudly.

"Here it is," Sidney said. He read the label out loud: 'Mr. Hero: The Perfect Artificial All-Purpose Champion of Truth and Justice.' That's all, folks," he said with a nod. "I'm out of here."

"Wait a minute," Daphne said. "What *is* that stuff?"

"I read you the label, didn't I?"

"Yeah," Daphne agreed, "but it didn't make any sense."

"You should be more careful who you make friends with," Sidney said to Harv.

"I'm curious, too," Harv admitted.

Sidney shook his head and strode toward the doorway.

Daphne blocked his way with her arm. She'd had enough of Sidney Agenda and his secrets. "We've seen a lot of strange stuff today, but this 'Mr. Hero' is the strangest yet. Before you leave I want to know what it is, and what kind of private school would think it's a good final project."

"Who died and made you sheriff?" Sidney asked. He seemed surprised by Daphne's outburst, but a little amused, too.

"Why don't you just tell us?" Harv asked.

For the first time Sidney smiled. "That's a very interesting question," Sidney admitted.

"Do you have an interesting answer?" Daphne asked.

Sidney glanced longingly at the door once or twice, but then he relaxed. "Can you vouch for her, Harv?" Sidney asked.

"I guess," Harv said. "She did just move in, though."

Sidney nodded slowly while he switched the jar from one hand to the other. It looked heavy. "If Harv says you're okay, you're okay." He shrugged. "Besides, the goons know most of this stuff anyway. My private school is Paladin Tech, a school for heroes started by my parents, Marvin and Agnes Agenda."

"I never heard of a school for heroes," Daphne said. As far as she was concerned, that was more goofiness.

"It's real, trust me," Sidney told her. "My mom and dad are generally off in some foreign place searching for exotic crime-fighting methods or opening new schools or acting as heroes. They always leave me with my aunt Millicent." He chuckled. "Though I'm never sure if maybe they don't leave her with me."

That last thing was the only part of Sidney's speech that made sense to Daphne. In her experience she and her dad took care of each other in about equal amounts. "Is your aunt Millicent married?" Daphne asked, always looking for a wife for her dad.

"Who wants to know?" Sidney asked.

Daphne smiled. She was getting used to Sidney's blunt way of talking and it bothered her less than it had. After all, she was not always little Miss Manners herself. "I'd like my dad—I'd like to meet her."

Sidney shrugged broadly. "Aunt Millicent and I moved to Paladin Tech," he explained, "which is in town behind an ice-cream shop. She doesn't come around here anymore, and I don't think either of you is likely to visit the school."

"You got that right, dude," Daphne grumbled.

"So, is the interrogation over?" Sidney asked.

Sidney was apparently a big talker, but Daphne had no way of knowing if his stories were true. The stuff in the jar might be a superhero, or it might be the world's largest wad of bubble gum. All the secret electronics might be no more useful than the props on the set of a science-fiction movie. Daphne was eager to find out.

She let Sidney out of the room, and he left with his jar. Before he reached the staircase, she'd already decided to take another look at the trapdoor that led to the River Thames.

She was surprised when Sidney stopped at the bottom of the stairs. "I got so busy working on Mr. Hero," he said, "that I was totally zonked when Aunt Millicent sold the house. She said she had permission from my parents, but I don't know. Sometimes Aunt Millicent's kind of a space cadet."

"Was she a space cadet this time?" Harv asked.

"Maybe not," Sidney said. "She thought we wouldn't be hassled as much if we lived at Paladin Tech instead of in a neighborhood." He shook his head. "If she'd told me we were moving, this entire trip to get my stuff wouldn't have been necessary."

Against her will, Daphne heard herself asking one more question. "Who'd hassle you?"

Sidney lowered his chin, raised a finger to his lips, and glanced around from side to side in a way Daphne thought was silly and exaggerated. "In the hero business you're either quick or you're dead," he said in hushed tones. Daphne decided Sidney was trying to scare them.

Suddenly five figures bolted into the front hall from the living room. They were dressed in black, like ninjas, but they were kid-size, no bigger than Daphne herself. She stared in surprise. Nothing like this ever happened in her old neighborhood.

One of the ninjas stepped forward and stuck out a hand. "You lose this time, Sidney," the ninja said. "Give me Mr. Hero."

THREE

Who Are Those Guys?

Sidney seemed more amused than astonished by the ninjas. "Hey, what is this, Lowell?" he asked. "Don't I rate a 'please'?" He shifted the jar to his other hand.

"Why waste it?" Lowell said. He motioned for one of the other ninjas to take the jar.

Sidney suddenly made a motion like a chicken flapping a wing, and the big yellow flower on his lapel squirted liquid over the five ninjas. The liquid began to smoke immediately, and the smell burned Daphne's nose and throat. While the ninjas coughed and tried to retreat, Sidney surprised Daphne by taking her hand. She grabbed Harv's.

"Come on!" Sidney cried and dragged the other two toward the front door. (Briefly she hoped the liquid Sidney used wouldn't stain the floors.) Then something crashed to the floor between them and the front door. It stank terribly, a cross between skunk and fertilizer.

They backed away, but were caught between

the stink and the recovering ninjas. Apparently, the liquid's effect lasted only a few minutes. Daphne and Harv were too confused to think, but Sidney turned and ran into the ninjas, his right arm out like that of a football player heading for a touchdown.

Ninjas grabbed at him, but something in Sidney's hand buzzed like an angry bee. The ninjas leaped back whenever Sidney touched them. In a moment Sidney, Harv, and Daphne were heading for the back of the house with Lowell and his ninjas not far behind.

Sidney dragged them into a broom closet and shut the door. They were unpleasantly jammed together. Sidney then pushed against the back wall, something clicked, and the wall slid open a crack. Frantically Sidney slipped his fingers into the crack and, with a sudden yank, slid the door open all the way.

They were mashed into a room that was even smaller than the closet. A computer screen surrounded by buttons, dials, and switches took up most of the space. Stars blinked toward them from the center of the screen. A fan in the ceiling hummed. Below the screen was a keyboard that contained hundreds of keys.

Sidney shoved the sliding door closed, and the three of them stood there listening to the ninjas moving around the house. From all the crashing and banging, they weren't being very careful with Daphne's stuff. She wondered if she shouldn't have stayed to protect her turf.

"What kind of machine is this?" Daphne asked.

Sidney didn't say anything.

"Come on," Daphne insisted. "It's my house."

Sidney grunted. "It's called a locator," he said. "You can find out where stuff is. Kind of an automated phone book."

"Handy," Harv agreed.

The little fan in the ceiling was humming along, but the air soon became warm and stale. The longer they stood there listening to each other breathe, the less afraid Daphne became and the more time she had to think.

The thing she realized was that the stuff in Sidney's jar might be as valuable as he claimed. Maybe it really was something called Mr. Hero. Now that the ninjas had arrived, Daphne was beginning to believe Sidney Agenda.

Sidney pulled the buzzer from his index finger and put it into a pocket.

"It looks to me," she whispered, "as if you guys get your equipment from the backs of comic books."

"Who are those guys?" Harv asked, whispering.

"They're Lowell Gravenstien and four of his friends," Sidney said. "They go to James Moriarty Preparatory School for Young Gentlemen and Ladies."

"That's a mouthful," Daphne said.

"Yeah," Sidney agreed. "That's why we usually call their school Moe Prep. They're crosstown rivals of Paladin Tech."

"In what?" Daphne asked.

"Everything. It gets kind of nasty sometimes."

"I can see that," Daphne said. "Why rivals?"

Sidney sighed. "All right, here's the way it is. Paladin Tech is a school for heroes. Moe Prep is a school for villains and evil geniuses."

Sidney seemed quite serious. And it all fit in with everything else that had happened. With a sinking feeling, Daphne wondered what she'd gotten into. It was all very exciting to watch this kind of stuff in a movie or read it in a book, but when somebody—like her—could really get hurt, it was more scary than exciting.

"If Lowell Gravenstien is a student at Moe Prep, I guess that makes him an evil genius," Harv said.

"You got that right. He wants to rule the world when he grows up. I figure he has a good shot at it, but that's not the worst."

"I can't wait," Daphne said.

Sidney glanced toward the door. He looked really worried. "Despite the fact that he's an evil genius, or maybe because of it," he explained, "Lowell Gravenstien is also sort of a dweeb. He's so polite to adults, it makes my teeth hurt. My aunt Millicent holds him up to me as a model of good deportment."

"Deportment?" Daphne asked.

"He must be *very* polite," Harv said.

"It's disgusting," Sidney assured them. "Shh!" He listened for a moment. "The ninjas are outside the closet!" he whispered.

A ninja girl opened the closet door. "Not in here," she said. The sound of crashing and banging and throwing things around went away.

Sidney pulled open the sliding door. The fresher air that came in was a relief. The ninjas were still in the house, but up on the second floor now.

"Time for us to make our daring escape," Sidney said, leading them through the house toward the front door.

Suddenly the ninjas were thundering down the front stairs. Sidney glanced around wildly. "We'll never make it," he whispered and handed the jar to Daphne.

She was so surprised she almost dropped it.

"Run back to the trapdoor," Sidney said to Daphne and Harv. He ran toward the stairway before Daphne had a chance to ask if the river below the house really was the Thames.

Daphne was about to follow Sidney, but Harv dragged her into the family room. He lifted the trapdoor and hurried them down. Daphne sat down on the cold stone steps as Harv lowered the trapdoor over them.

She breathed through her mouth while they sat there in the dark. The smell was almost as rotten as the stuff in the stink bomb the ninjas had thrown. The only light came from around the edges of the trapdoor. The light glistened a little on the gently swirling oily black water below. Above them, they could hear Lowell Gravenstien shouting Sidney Agenda's name and laughing like a crazy person.

"Sidney's a brave guy, I guess," Harv said.

"Yeah," Daphne agreed. "I hope this jar is worth all the trouble."

Soon it grew quiet above, and Daphne couldn't stand sitting in the sour-smelling darkness any longer. "I got the idea that Sidney thought we should make our escape along the river," Daphne said.

Harv followed her gaze down to the water and shrugged. "That was the idea I got, too," he said. "But do we go upstream or downstrcam? What if the water divides? I think the ninjas are gone, so maybe we're better off going back upstairs."

Daphne decided that Harv was right. She climbed the steps and pushed the trapdoor up a little. Hearing nothing, she climbed the rest of the way out, still lugging the jar. A loud whirring noise started up in the backyard.

Daphne and Harv ran to the kitchen door just in time to see the five ninjas pile onto a strange-looking flying machine with Sidney Agenda. Sidney was bound in heavy ropes.

Daphne was astonished. Even on a day as filled with wonders as this one, Lowell Gravenstien's flying machine was special. A gondola shaped like a swan hung beneath a long narrow hot-air balloon with points at each end. The heads of bearded men with puffed-out cheeks blowing wind were painted around it. Beneath the swan gondola three ninjas pedaled furiously to make a pair of propellers turn, which pushed the whole contraption forward as if it were some kind of air boat. It rose quickly and disappeared among the clouds.

"I don't know about you, Daf," Harv said, "but I believe everything Sidney told us."

Daphne could only agree. Mr. Hero suddenly seemed a lot heavier.

FOUR

One More Ice-Cream Cone

Daphne's new responsibility dismayed her. She set the jar on the kitchen table and stared at it glumly.

The jar was the same size it had been, of course, but it took up a lot more space in her life. She certainly had the option of ignoring the challenge the jar represented, of walking away from it, of burying it in the backyard, or of pouring the contents down the sink, but she'd still have to deal with Lowell Gravenstien. She was sure now that nothing would prevent him from returning for the jar if he didn't get what he wanted out of Sidney.

"We have to save Sidney from Lowell," Daphne said to Harv. Being one of the two people in the world who knew Sidney had been kidnapped, she felt a certain responsibility for saving him. Still, if Lowell Gravenstien really was an evil genius—which seemed likely—she knew she wasn't qualified to handle him alone.

"What do you mean, *we?*" Harv asked.

"Go home if you want to," Daphne said. "I guess I was wrong. I thought you were someone who could be counted on in a pinch."

"I am, generally. But this is not your average school-yard hassle."

"True," Daphne admitted. "We need help."

They both glanced at the jar. Daphne read the label again—"Mr. Hero: The Perfect Artificial All-Purpose Champion of Truth and Justice."

"It's just what we need," Daphne said.

"We don't know how it works," Harv reminded her. "Or even *if* it works."

"We're going to have to take some chances soon, or we might as well leave the jar on the front step and forget about Sidney," Daphne said.

Harv nodded. "I'd just like to try something less weird than depending on a jar of purple glop."

Daphne could see his point. "What about Sidney's aunt Millicent?" she suggested.

"We'd have to find Paladin Tech," Harv said, "but we don't have much to go on. Sidney said it's behind an ice-cream shop in town."

"Sidney never mentioned anything else to you when he lived next door?"

"No. I never even heard of Paladin Tech before today."

"We need a telephone book," Harv said, trying to be helpful.

"I don't know if we have one," Daphne said, thinking. Then it occurred to her that they didn't need a phone book; they could use the locator Sidney had shown them. She suggested it to Harv.

"Is that a good idea?" Harv asked.

"It's a great idea," Daphne assured him, though she wasn't really convinced.

They went back into the broom closet at the back of the house, and Daphne clicked open the secret panel. The tiny room was a lot less cramped with only two people inside.

"I'd rather use a phone book," Harv said as he warily studied the machinery. "I could get one from home, you know."

"Let's try a few things first," Daphne said. She knew a little about computers because her old school had some that students could use.

She pushed the ENTER key, and immediately the stars went away, leaving behind a list of choices. She used the arrow keys to move a lighted bar down to TELEPHONE DIRECTORY. She pushed the ENTER key again, and the machine asked what locale they were interested in.

Daphne typed *downtown,* the machine continued to ask them questions, and they gave it the best answers they could. The program was a no-brainer.

The computer had no entry for Paladin Tech. "You probably need a security code to get it," Harv said.

"Let's try ice-cream shops, then," Daphne said. She was delighted when she was able to get the computer to display a list of them.

"I told you," Daphne said. "Hundreds of them."

"That's not hundreds," Harv said.

"Okay," Daphne admitted. "I exaggerated." There were fifteen or twenty ice-cream shops. She told the machine to print a copy of the list, and it dispensed a thin slippery-feeling sheet of paper through a slot.

"All we need now is a telephone," Daphne said. "My dad said ours won't be connected until tomorrow."

"Don't look at me," Harv said. "We have a phone, but it's always busy."

"Maybe we can dial out on this thing," Daphne said and began to play with the machine again. She quickly found a telephone option and used it to dial All Flavors Ice Cream. While the number rang, worry crept up on her again. She pushed it away. She'd made up her mind to help Sidney, and she knew she wouldn't be able to look herself in the mirror if she wimped out now.

"All Flavors Ice Cream," a speaker in the

wall said. "This week's flavor is Pumpkin Ripple."

"Do you know where I can find Paladin Tech?" Daphne asked. Such a long silence followed that Daphne came to suspect that the man hadn't heard her.

She was about to ask again, louder, when the man at All Flavors Ice Cream spoke. "What was that flavor again?" he asked.

"It's not a flavor," Daphne explained patiently. "It's a school."

There was another long silence. "Never heard of it," the guy said and hung up.

Daphne glanced at Harv, who shrugged, so she called the second number.

By the time they reached the last name on the list, Zinkwafer's Frozen Treats, and got pretty much the same answer, Daphne was discouraged.

"There's no such place," she stated. "Sidney lied."

"What about the ninjas?" Harv asked. "What about Mr. Hero and all the trapdoors and equipment and stuff?"

Daphne suggested a few other explanations: Sidney and Lowell were just two rich kids playing. Or maybe this whole situation was being taped for *Weird Videos,* a TV show. None of these answers seemed very likely. As a matter of fact, she found the most likely explanation to be the one Sidney had given them. She and Harv should be taking this situation a lot more seriously, she decided.

"You know what I think?" Daphne said. "I think we're approaching this all wrong."

"What do you mean?"

"I mean, if you were a secret school for heroes, would you admit it to some kid on the phone?"

"I guess not," Harv said.

"We'll have to visit these places and see for ourselves," Daphne said.

While Daphne wrote a note for her dad, Harv went next door to tell his parents where he was going. "They say each of their kids is precious," Harv explained when he got back, "but sometimes it takes a while before they notice one of us is missing. In this case, I want them to notice right away."

"You think we'll need saving?" Daphne asked.

"I think we should have our heads examined," Harv said. He took her to the bus stop, where they waited to go downtown.

While they rode, Daphne held the jar of Mr. Hero in her lap, and Harv studied the list. He planned their route and with a stubby pencil put a number next to the name of each ice-cream shop. They would make a big circle through downtown and, after hitting all the ice-cream shops, return to where they'd started. Since they had so few clues, Daphne agreed that it was as good a plan as any.

They got off the bus in an industrial part of town. They saw a lot of big buildings that were nothing more than block-long sheds. Huge trucks rumbled by over the potholed street.

"Are you sure about this?" Daphne asked.

"If this address is right, I'm sure."

They walked down a long hot block—the jar becoming heavier by the moment—and came to a place called Raff Distributing, which was not an ice-cream shop but a parking lot for Eskimo Taco ice-cream trucks. When they entered the office, a fat woman behind a battered gray metal desk asked, "Can I help you?"

"We're looking for a place called Paladin Tech," Daphne said. "It's kind of a school."

"Was that you who called before?" she asked accusingly.

Daphne realized with a shock that at many of the places they were about to visit, she would be speaking to the same person she'd already spoken to on the phone.

"Yes, ma'am," Daphne said.

"This is a business," the woman said. "I'm

not here to play games." She sighed. "I told you there's a church nearby, but no schools that I know about."

Daphne and Harv waited for her to say more.

"Is there anything else?" she asked impaticntly.

"No, thank you," Daphne said and pulled Harv back outside. She was frustrated, but if she'd stayed in the office any longer, she would have just gotten angry. Daphne hated it when adults thought they could be rude to kids just because they were kids.

"On to the next place!" she cried.

Harv studied the list. "That way," he said, pointing.

Two blocks away they found an old-fashioned shop called Fenton's Creamery. They each had a cone. Daphne's was vanilla, her favorite. The ice cream was cold and delicious. Unfortunately, Fenton's Creamery was not the right shop.

They had another cone each at the second shop, but by the third one, Daphne didn't want any more. Her throat was frozen, and she could feel her teeth decaying from all the sweetness. They argued about which of them had to order a cone.

"Okay," Harv finally said, "I'll have one this time if you have one at the next place."

"Okay," Daphne agreed, hoping the place

they were in, the Chocolate Cow, was the link to Paladin Tech. It wasn't.

The fourth place was called Uncle Alexander's Ice Cream. It was a long narrow room with an ice-cream freezer running along one side and red plastic booths down the other. Daphne ordered a vanilla cone, and the soda jerk went right to work, scooping deep into the vanilla tub. When she casually asked about Paladin Tech, he kept scooping—he had dug out quite a large scoop by then—but glanced at her suspiciously, as if she'd just offered to sell him a hot watch.

Daphne was excited to think that this might be the right place, but she refused to get her hopes up. Maybe the guy was just naturally suspicious.

"What kind of a place is Paladin Tech?" the soda jerk asked.

"It's a kind of a school," Harv said.

"School?" the soda jerk asked as if he'd never heard the word before.

"You know," said Harv. "A place where they teach you stuff. Like how to be heroic, for instance."

The soda jerk nodded. He handed the ice-cream cone to Daphne. It was so large by now, it looked like a softball sitting on the cone. "This is on the house," he said. "You're our fiftieth customer today."

Daphne tried to act casual, though she suspected that they'd hit the right ice-cream shop at last. "Oh, is that so," she said. "Very interesting."

"The boss will be here soon. He'll want pictures. Why don't you wait in a booth?"

"Okay," Daphne said. She and Harv exchanged glances and headed for a booth near the door.

"No. Not that one," the soda jerk said. "Over there." He pointed to the back of the shop.

Daphne and Harv walked to the booth, where they found a table covered with half-empty milkshakes, melted ice cream, and soggy napkins. People wouldn't sit there unless they had to.

"Here?" Harv asked.

"Right there," the soda jerk said. "It won't be a moment."

They both slid into one side—the seat on the other side had melted ice cream all over it—and put the jar on the seat between them. The ice cream in Daphne's cone was beginning to melt. She stood it up in one of the milkshake glasses. She didn't really want it.

A moment later the soda jerk reached for a big lever that said Moxie on it. Daphne had heard that Moxie was an old-time soft drink but she'd never tasted it. He pulled the Moxie lever twice, and the entire booth began to rotate.

FIVE

We Were Heroic When We Left Here

The booth spun them into a large room with chrome paneling about halfway up each wall. Above the chrome hung dark shapes that depicted the skyline of a great city. The air had a cold artificial smell, as if it had been recycled many times through an air-conditioning system.

Across from them, a woman sat behind a desk. On her shirt pocket she wore a yellow plastic triangle printed with the number fifty-two. She smiled. "Welcome to Paladin Tech, kids."

Daphne felt wonderful that she and Harv had been able to find Paladin Tech using only the flimsiest of clues. Their success also meant that Mr. Hero would soon be off their hands and Sidney would be that much closer to being rescued. The thought relieved her, but it made her sad, too. After this she and Harv would have to go back to real life.

Number Fifty-two took their fingerprints and had each of them sit in front of a machine that flashed light into their eyes. "We're checking your retinal patterns," she told them.

"What does that mean?" Harv asked.

"Everybody in the world has a different pattern of blood vessels on the backs of his or her eyeballs. Comparing your pattern to the patterns we have on file is the most modern way to positively identify you."

"You have our retinal patterns on file?" Harv asked, astonished.

Number Fifty-two smiled. "I want to congratulate both of you," she said, instead of answering Harv's question. "Finding the school is our entrance exam. If you are cleared by security, you're in."

"Suppose we don't want to be in?" Daphne asked.

The question seemed to bewilder Number Fifty-two. "Then why are you here?" she asked.

Daphne momentarily wondered if they should tell. Theoretically, they were all on the same side. Besides, time was important. They could not just take classes and hope to run into Sidney's aunt eventually.

"We're here to see Sidney Agenda's aunt Millicent," Daphne said. "About this." She held up the jar.

"Millicent Kuryakin?" Number Fifty-two asked.

"I guess," Daphne said.

"What's in the jar?" Number Fifty-two asked.

"Sidney Agenda's project," Harv said.

Number Fifty-two thought about that till the computer on her desk began to chime, and she went around to see what the problem was. She smiled. "I'm delighted to report that both of you passed our security check with flying colors. Are you certain you don't want to register as students?" Two triangles of plastic rolled out of the computer's printer. She held them while Daphne and Harv considered their answer.

"Maybe," Harv said.

Daphne could see that he was intrigued by the possibility of becoming a hero. Actually, she was, too. On TV, and in books and movies, the hero was always the most awesome character. Terrible things could happen to him or her, but the hero always triumphed in the end. Triumphing would be nice, especially if it was for a good cause.

Daphne refused to be sidetracked, though. "Right now we'd like to see Millicent Kuryakin," she said.

"Very well," Number Fifty-two said with obvious disappointment. "But it's not every day we get two such likely candidates." She handed each of them a yellow triangle. Daphne clipped on number two-hundred-three, and Harv clipped on number two-hundred-four.

"You'll have to leave the jar out here."

"I thought we were cleared," Harv said.

"*You* are cleared," Number Fifty-two explained. "But we don't know what's in the jar."

"I'm not going anywhere without this jar," Daphne stated.

"Me, either," Harv said.

Looking worried, Number Fifty-two sat down behind her desk and whispered for a few moments into a telephone. Daphne tried to remain calm, but her anger was growing by the second. She and Harv were trying to do somebody a favor, but adults kept getting in their way.

Number Fifty-two smiled. "Security approves the jar," she said with triumph.

"Thank you," Harv said.

Daphne just grumbled.

A trumpet fanfare blared from somewhere, and the room suddenly went black. Daphne grabbed Harv's hand and held on tight. A man appeared in a spotlight on the roofs of the fake skyline, dwarfing the fake buildings. He was dressed in a white form-fitting suit with one green band around his chest and another around his waist. He wore green boots that came almost to his knees. He had big green multifaceted eyes, like a bug.

"Way cool," Harv said. Daphne admired Harv for his calm. If she had brothers and sisters, maybe she would be calm, too, she reflected.

The man casually held a length of rope that dangled from the ceiling. He leaped into the air, swung over them, and dropped lightly between them and the desk. Clipped to his sleeve was a yellow triangle with the number seventy-three on it.

The lights came on again, and Daphne fought the urge to applaud.

"This is Number Seventy-three," Number Fifty-two said. "He will take you to Ms. Kuryakin."

A chrome door behind Number Fifty-two's desk slid open with a quiet *shush.* Number Seventy-three walked to the door and motioned for them to come with him.

Almost afraid of what would happen next, Daphne and Harv followed Number Seventy-three through the doorway under a sign that said WE WERE HEROIC WHEN WE LEFT HERE. The chrome door slid shut behind them with a finality that was alarming. They started down a long hallway.

Daphne forgot her fear as she was distracted by the sights. The walls of the hallway were glass, and through them Daphne saw men and women working at computer terminals.

Then there were adults rushing around in what appeared to be costumes. Daphne saw them dressed in space suits, cowboy outfits complete with white Stetson hats and fringe, green Robin Hood tunics and tights, and the occasional trench coat. Harv pointed out a guy who was dressed like Sherlock Holmes in a cape and deerstalker cap.

Daphne knew a hero when she saw one—any kid did—and this place was jammed with them. They were probably the teachers, she decided, instructing the next generation in the business of saving the world.

Farther on was a wonderful obstacle course where students practiced climbing up, over, and under hurdles. Some were pursued by the teachers who were armed with six-shooters, crossbows, or ray guns, each dressed appropriately for the weapon carried.

One minute they were walking along the hallway, and the next, glass wall panels slid aside, admitting a band of ninjas who quickly surrounded them. The ninjas carried long sticks that they jabbed at Daphne, Harv, and Number Seventy-three.

Lowell Gravenstien and his gang from Moe Prep had invaded Paladin Tech!

SIX

The Main Nerve

Number Seventy-three swung around and, with a series of swift high kicks, knocked the sticks from the ninjas' hands. Then, while they were still dazed, he grabbed one of the ninjas as if he meant to throw him at the others.

Daphne was frightened, though Harv seemed calm.

One of the ninjas pulled off her mask to reveal a girl Daphne's own age. "We surrender, Mr. Flyeyes!" she cried.

To Daphne's surprise, Number Seventy-three smiled and gently put down the ninja. The other kid ninjas pulled off their masks.

"Good try," Number Seventy-three said. "But don't assume because you outnumber an enemy you've automatically won."

"We didn't assume," one of the kids said. "We just didn't expect you to kick away our sticks."

"Ah," Number Seventy-three said. "If you're going to be a hero, you have to be ready for anything. Have a look at Chapter Twenty-seven of *Heroes Then and Now.* We'll talk about it in class tomorrow."

Apparently, being a hero took a lot more practice than Daphne had supposed.

Chattering among themselves, the ninjas swarmed down the hall and disappeared through a door. Number Seventy-three urged Daphne and Harv to move along.

Daphne poked Harv with her elbow. "How did you know they weren't really ninjas?"

"It was logical," Harv said and shrugged. "It didn't make sense that bad guys could get this far into a place like Paladin Tech without tripping an alarm."

"Very good," Number Seventy-three said. "You seem to have a talent for this sort of thing."

"Not necessarily," Daphne said. "He just has a lot of brothers and sisters."

"I see," Number Seventy-three said. "This way."

He led them to the far end of the hallway, where he opened the double doors and showed them into a big office. Number Seventy-three said, "Wait here, please." With a smile and a wave he shut the doors and left them alone.

Daphne gripped the jar tighter as she looked around.

Most of the office was taken up by a big round table surrounded by rolling armchairs. Maps on the walls blinked with different colored lights. In one corner of the room sat a locator much like the one in the broom closet in Daphne's house.

"We've struck the main nerve," Daphne said.

Harv nodded, apparently as impressed by the room as she was.

On a table to one side lay a copy of the Paladin Tech catalog. Daphne set the jar down so she could flip through it. In addition to the usual courses, like history and math, she saw some pretty unusual ones.

"Look at this," she said to Harv. " 'Packing Your Clothing With Spy Devices one-oh-one,' and 'Getting Along with Your Evil Adversary two-hundred-A.' "

Harv peeked over her shoulder. "Huh?" he said. " 'When and How to Use Your Theme Music three-oh-five.' I don't have theme music. Do you?"

"Maybe we would if we went here," Daphne suggested. She wondered if her own theme music would sound like what she heard on TV and in the movies. Would she have to write it herself?

A door slid open at the back of the room. Daphne dropped the catalog as a tall and imposing woman entered. She was dressed in a tailored navy blue suit with a white collar. Her hair was a beautiful silver and seemed to be sculpted. Half-glasses perched on her nose. The only thing about her that wasn't in perfect classic taste was the yellow triangle clipped to her collar. It had the number three on it.

Without looking at them, she sat at the big round table and gave it a small push to the right. It turned, bringing a folder around to her. She glanced at the folder through her half-glasses.

The woman was a little older than Daphne's dad, but Daphne wondered whether she would make a good wife.

"I hope," the woman said, "that you're here to fix the photocopying machine."

"No, ma'am," Daphne said. She felt as though she were in school. The woman had the air of a teacher, or worse yet, a vice-principal. "We're here to tell you about your nephew, Sidney." She picked up the jar, ready to explain.

The woman gaped at Daphne and Harv as if they'd suggested she fly to the moon on gossamer wings.

"Are we in the right room?" Harv asked. "We're looking for Sidney's aunt Millicent Kuryakin."

"I am she. If you're not here to fix the photocopier, you must be the ones who have been using the pencils for personal reasons. I must ask you to stop or face the consequences."

"No, ma'am," Harv said. "We're not here about the pencils. We just got here."

Daphne disliked being accused of things, especially by strangers. This woman ran a tight ship, and Daphne decided she didn't want a mother who was quite so *organized.* "How can you talk about pencils when Sidney is in trouble?" Daphne asked, exasperated.

Aunt Millicent glared at them. "Don't use that tone with me, young lady," she said. "Pencils are the backbone of any company."

Daphne thought she had better apologize, so she said, "I'm sorry," despite the fact she didn't really feel she'd done anything wrong.

"Now, what about Sidney?" Aunt Millicent asked with a touch of irritation.

At last, Daphne thought with relief. "Your nephew Sidney Agenda has been abducted by Lowell Gravenstien," she said. "He left this jar with us. We'd like to leave it with you."

"What does it contain?" she asked, wrinkling her nose.

"It's Sidney's final project for his Methods of Crime Fighting class," Daphne said.

"Mr. Hero," Harv explained.

"I see. You say that Sidney was abducted?"

"Yes," Daphne said. She and Harv went on to explain what had happened, starting with Sidney's first appearance on the wall of the house and telling the whole story right up to the moment when he'd been taken away by Lowell Gravenstien and the ninjas in their strange hot-air balloon.

Aunt Millicent continued to stare silently at them after they had finished. "Sidney's parents will not like this," she said at last.

"Probably not," Daphne said. "What about Sidney?"

"What *about* Sidney?" she asked a little impatiently. "If he's playing with Lowell Gravenstien, then I assure you he is in good hands."

"Playing?" Daphne exclaimed.

"Good hands?" Harv asked.

"Of course. Lowell Gravenstien is such a well-behaved little gentleman. He has probably taken Sidney to Moriarty Prep, where the game they're playing will no doubt be concluded. If you wish to join in the fun, have a good time. I ask only that you play nicely."

"That's it?" Daphne asked, astonished.

"There is nothing more important than good sportsmanship," Aunt Millicent said. "Have I missed something?"

Daphne wanted to say that she had missed

everything. For a moment she considered trying to explain again. Maybe different words would help. But judging by Aunt Millicent's interests in photocopiers, pencils, and sportsmanship, Daphne doubted if any words could convince her that Sidney was in real trouble. She also doubted that leaving the Mr. Hero jar with the woman would be safe. Aunt Millicent might just throw it away, or worse yet, leave it around where somebody from Moe Prep could pick it up.

"I guess not," Daphne said.

"So," Harv said casually, "if you'd just tell us where Moe Prep is, we'll be on our way."

Daphne glanced at him with amazement. She was miffed that she hadn't thought to ask that.

"That wouldn't be sporting," Aunt Millicent said.

"But we want to play the game," Daphne explained.

"Exactly," Aunt Millicent said. "One of your objects as players is to find Moe Prep. Merely telling you where it is would give you an unfair advantage. I couldn't allow that."

"I suppose not," Daphne said glumly. "Sorry to have bothered you. Come on, Harv."

"No bother," Aunt Millicent said and spun the table once again.

As Daphne crossed to the double doors, she decided to ask somebody else where Moe Prep was located. Aunt Millicent couldn't be the only person who knew.

Just as she was thinking this, the floor opened under her and Harv, and suddenly they were falling. She gripped the Mr. Hero jar and screamed. They fell a couple of feet onto a slick metal slide that curved up on either side of them. Still screaming, Daphne slid down and down so fast she couldn't get her breath. She heard the echoes of Harv screaming behind her.

She landed with a soft thump on a big pillow. She was pleased that she had enough presence of mind to roll out of the way in time for Harv to land.

"Come on, kids," a pleasant-looking man said as he plucked off their yellow tags and pulled them to their feet.

"Do you know where Moe Prep is?" Daphne asked as she was hustled to a tiny elevator.

"Yes, I do," the man said and pushed the Up button.

The doors *shooshed* closed, and Daphne felt the floor push up at her as the elevator rocketed them upward.

A moment later the elevator stopped so suddenly that Daphne almost lost all the ice cream she'd eaten that afternoon. She and Harv were

MR HERO

crammed inside a telephone booth at the edge of an alley. An OUT OF ORDER sign hung from the coin box.

"Out of order my foot!" Daphne cried. She ran out of the alley. "Which way to the ice-cream parlor?" she asked.

Harv glanced up and down the street. "That way," he said. They ran. Daphne was determined to find Moe Prep's location.

The same soda jerk was still standing behind the counter of Uncle Alexander's Ice Cream. He looked at Daphne and Harv as if he'd never seen them before. "What'll it be, kids?" he asked.

"Where's Moe Prep?" Daphne asked.

"Who?" the soda jerk asked.

Daphne understood that she wouldn't be getting anything out of this guy. She grabbed Harv and pulled him back to the dirty booth.

They sat there for a while, Harv patiently, Daphne expecting that any moment the soda jerk would pull the Moxie lever. But all the soda jerk did was stare at them occasionally while he wiped down the other tables.

"How long are we going to sit here?" Harv asked.

"Until we get some answers," Daphne said.

But soon Daphne couldn't tolerate sitting any longer. She got up and gave the soda jerk a dirty look as she stomped out. She stood outside the shop angrily shifting the jar from hand to hand. She saw nothing but trouble in her future. If they couldn't get the help of the Paladin Tech people, she and Harv would have to save Sidney by themselves, a job she didn't relish.

When Harv strolled out, Daphne handed the jar to him. "Here," she said. "You carry it for a while. If we're going to save Sidney, we'll likely need the help of the 'Perfect Champion of Truth and Justice.' " She was still not convinced that the jar was worth all this trouble.

They walked up the street to the bus stop. A moment later Harv said, "Maybe Aunt Millicent is right. Maybe Sidney and Lowell are just playing a game."

Daphne had disliked Aunt Millicent so thoroughly that this hadn't even occurred to her. She thought about it now. "Sidney seemed pretty frightened," she said.

"He did," Harv agreed. "But that may have been part of the game. There's only one way to find out what's really going on."

Daphne knew he was right. "But if we rescue Sidney and it turns out this really is a game," she said, "I'm going to murder him myself."

SEVEN

The Thing in the Backyard

Because they'd found Paladin Tech, they didn't have to complete their tour of the ice-cream shops. *And,* Daphne realized gladly, they didn't have to eat any more ice cream. She and Harv just took the bus back to their neighborhood, then walked to Daphne's house.

"I think we ought to open the jar," Daphne said.

"But it might explode," Harv said. "And Sidney might not want us to open it."

"True," Daphne said, putting her hands on her hips. "And it might crawl out and eat us. What do you suggest?"

Harv shrugged. "We open it, I guess."

They went around to the two cement steps that led down from Daphne's family room to her backyard. Daphne set the Mr. Hero jar down on the top step.

"Ready?" she asked.

"No. But go ahead."

Daphne wiped her hands on her jeans, then

tried to unscrew the lid. "It's moving!" she cried. She held the jar closed for a moment while she let her courage build, then pulled the lid off.

They both leaned forward and watched.

Inside, the purple stuff just sat there, smooth as grape ice cream. Slowly Daphne put out a finger and touched it. It felt soft and yielding, neither cold nor warm.

"What does it feel like?" Harv asked.

"Not much." She wiped her hand on her jeans, feeling like an idiot. She wasn't sure what she'd been expecting, but it seemed unlikely that this purple stuff would be of any use to them.

Then all at once an awful sour smell wafted out of the jar.

"Yow," Daphne said, waving it away. "It smells worse than that stink bomb."

"Maybe it went bad," Harv suggested.

"Maybe it never was any good," Daphne said grumpily.

"When my parents open a bottle of wine for a party," Harv said, "they let it sit for a while before anybody drinks it. Mom says it's called letting the wine breathe. Maybe this stuff needs to breathe."

"Maybe," Daphne said doubtfully.

"Right," Harv said. He stood up. "If it still

smells like that in the morning," he said, "I think we should get rid of it. I don't care how good a hero it is."

"Okay," Daphne agreed.

"See you later," Harv said. "I've got to get home."

After Harv left, Daphne watched the purple stuff for a while longer. Nothing happened, so she finally went into the house and started unpacking the kitchen stuff. She had found the can opener by dinnertime and opened a couple of cans of baked beans to warm up. By the time her dad got home, she had set up another picnic on the living room floor. It wasn't as much fun as the first one, and Daphne decided to get the table set up as soon as possible.

"So," Mr. Trusk asked between bites, "anything happen today?"

"I met the kids next door," Daphne said. "They seem nice."

"You see?" Mr. Trusk said. "You'll like living in this neighborhood. I know I do. I have a date for tonight."

Daphne was delighted. "What's her name?"

"Brigid LeBlanc. I met her at work, and we're going to a movie."

"Is she wife material?" Daphne asked.

"I don't know," Mr. Trusk said. "I just met her."

"Can I meet her?"

"All right. But don't be a nuisance."

Daphne frowned. "I can act like a grown-up when it's necessary, Dad."

"I know. I just don't want you proposing for me."

That made them both laugh.

After dinner Mr. Trusk went upstairs to get ready for his date, and Daphne washed the dishes. When she was done, she went up to her room for a while. It had been a long day, and she was glad to spend a little time alone.

She was reading the copy of *Treasure Island* her dad had read as a boy. It had been given to him by *his* dad. The back cover said it was a "boy's book." In the olden days, when her grandfather had been a kid, girls were encouraged to read books about nurses who fell in love and other boring stuff. Daphne was glad that those days were over. Pirates were much more interesting than little girls who made it their life's work to be polite and proper.

Daphne sat on the window seat where Sidney had found his jar. The sky was dark and she could hear somebody practicing the violin next door at Harv's house. The violinist didn't play well, or even with much enthusiasm, but the notes floating up made Daphne feel cozy. This was a new neighborhood and it had been a strange day, but now normal people were doing normal things. Except for the violin music and the occasional rustle of leaves, all was quiet.

Then she heard a strange sound and became tense, listening. Something was moving around in her backyard. Had Lowell Gravenstien returned? Daphne hastily turned out the lamp and pushed the window open all the way. She strained to hear. The night air tasted cool and fragrant with the heady smells of summer flowers. Someone or something was edging through the heavy brush at the far end of the yard.

With the light off in her room, she could see the backyard a little better, but it was still a confusion of broad shadows. Hundreds of ninjas could be hiding out there.

The noise came again, and she thought she saw a bird the size of an ostrich stepping delicately through the undergrowth. It had a purple sheen. In the dim light she couldn't be sure. The bird was lost in shadow for a moment, and when it reappeared it looked less like a bird and more like a tree that had decided to go for a walk.

Daphne was confused and more than a little frightened. Compared to the weird stuff going on in her new backyard, heroes in a jar and kid ninjas were as comfortable as old shoes. It occurred to her then that the purple sheen she had seen in the backyard was the same color as the stuff in Sidney's jar. The thought that it could be wandering around her backyard made her uneasy.

Daphne carefully closed the window.

"I am calm," she told herself as she ran downstairs.

Down in the foyer she found her dad talking to a woman. Daphne frowned slightly. Although the lady was younger than Aunt Millicent, and prettier, she was also stiff and businesslike. Her hair was drawn back in a tight bun, and she was dressed as perfectly as a mannequin in a department store.

"Oh, Daf, I was just about to call you," her dad said. "This is Brigid LeBlanc."

Brigid LeBlanc smiled and held out her hand. Daphne shook it briefly. "Nice to meet you," Daphne said, remembering her manners.

Then she turned to her father. "Dad," she said, "something's in the backyard."

"What sort of something?" He looked at his date and smiled. "Kids," he said.

Daphne hated it when he did that. Kids were just as bright as most adults and smarter than some.

"I don't know," Daphne said, all the time realizing how ridiculous she sounded. "Sometimes it looks like a bird and sometimes it looks like a tree. It's big and purple."

"The child is overstimulated," Brigid LeBlanc said.

"I am not overstimulated," Daphne said coldly. "I saw something in the backyard."

Mr. Trusk set a hand on the woman's shoulder. "I'll be right back," he said and followed Daphne through the family room to the door leading outside.

"What's this about, Daf?" Mr. Trusk asked when they were alone.

"Something is out there," Daphne said. She opened the door and peered this way and that. Nothing happened. Even the violin playing had stopped.

"It's not there now," Mr. Trusk said. He shook his head. "Maybe you're too young for *Treasure Island.*"

Daphne sighed. "I'm not seeing pirates, Dad. *Treasure Island* has nothing to do with it."

"All right." He ruffled her hair. "I know I shouldn't leave you alone so much," he said. "First I'm at work all day, and now this date thing."

Her father was sweet, but he'd obviously missed the fact that *she'd* been taking care of *him* most of her life.

"You need a social life, Dad," she said. "I know that. Don't worry."

"I'll be fine," she said. "Have a good time."

Daphne returned to her room and turned out the light so she could see the dark yard better. She waited. She strained against the silence so hard that when the noise began again, it made her jump.

Something was definitely moving around there. It seemed to be a bird again. Or maybe not. Actually, it seemed to be more of a duck. Daphne's curiosity overcame her fear, and she went downstairs to the kitchen, where she found the barbecue tools in a box on the porch. The long fork was normally used to turn meat and toast marshmallows, but it made a reassuring weapon in her hand. If anything attacked her, it would find itself firmly poked.

She went outside and crept around to the steps at the back of the house. The Mr. Hero jar was empty. Lowell Gravenstien would have stolen the whole jar rather than empty it. That meant that Mr. Hero had probably crawled off by himself. Which meant that the purple creature Daphne had seen must be Mr. Hero. She could understand it expanding like a sponge once it was no longer restricted by the jar, but that didn't explain why it looked like a bird, then a tree, and then a duck.

She peered into the backyard. Something else was moving among the bushes at the far edge.

MR
HERO

What was it? Her barbecue fork suddenly seemed like a very flimsy weapon.

Somebody grabbed her from behind, and she let out a small yelp. As she struggled, the barbecue fork waved around in front of her like a fishing pole.

"Where is it?" a harsh voice whispered into her ear.

"Where's what?" she asked. The voice seemed familiar, though she couldn't place it from the few words she'd heard.

"The jar. Mr. Hero."

"The jar's over on the step if you want it. But it's empty."

A cat bounded out of a shadow and stared at them. It was the size of a big dog, but it looked more like a house cat—a longhaired purple house cat.

Frantically Daphne wondered whose side it was on.

EIGHT

Mr. Hero

"Let her go," the cat said, astonishing Daphne not only because it had spoken, but because it seemed to be speaking in her very own voice. Daphne stopped struggling, momentarily stunned.

"Hah," her attacker said. Daphne hoped he was just showing off.

"Let her go," the cat said again. It sat down and yawned broadly, showing its many sharp teeth.

The teeth must have convinced whoever was holding Daphne because suddenly he let go of her. Daphne jumped away and whirled around. She pointed the barbecue fork at him—a kid-size ninja like the ones who'd attacked the house earlier.

The ninja ignored the barbecue fork. "You haven't heard the last of Lowell Gravenstien!" he cried. Turning, he sprinted down the driveway and vanished into the shadows.

"Let her go," the cat said again.

Daphne turned back to the cat, surprised. "Is that all you can say?" she asked. She studied the cat, feeling like Alice in Wonderland.

"No, but it's fun. Let *her* go," the cat said, experimenting. "Let her *go. Let* her go."

Daphne laughed. The oversize cat was cute. Better yet, it showed no sign of wanting to eat her.

"You're Mr. Hero?" she said as a question.

"I am?" the cat said and scratched itself. "I am," it stated.

"Did Sidney Agenda really invent you?"

"That's what he told me."

Daphne had no doubt now that Sidney Agenda was a genius. Knowing that Mr. Hero was real made it more important than ever that she rescue Sidney from Moe Prep and Lowell Gravenstien.

Then the cat started to melt. It didn't just melt into a puddle, but into the shape of a duck, similar to the ones she'd discovered that afternoon.

"That's pretty good," Daphne said. "But can't you make yourself any smaller? More like a real duck?"

The duck looked down at itself. "No, just one size," it said, still sounding like Daphne. "I was glad to get out of that jar."

"I'll bet," Daphne said. She decided that this

creature wasn't really the *perfect* champion of truth and justice if it had to speak in her voice and couldn't change its size. "How did you end up with my voice?" Daphne asked.

"I have to talk like somebody," the duck said. "I haven't heard many people so far." Suddenly its voice changed. " 'You haven't seen the last of Lowell Gravenstien,' " it said so realistically that Daphne glanced around to see if the ninja had returned. " 'Who wants to know?' " it asked in Sidney Agenda's voice.

If Mr. Hero had to copy things, it was logical that it had taken the form of a cat with all the examples next door.

Even if Mr. Hero wasn't *perfect,* it seemed friendly. "You better come into the house," Daphne said. "Lowell Gravenstien might come back with friends."

"What does he want?" Mr. Hero asked, following her. It moved like a two-legged cat, not like a waddling duck.

"He wants you," Daphne told it.

"Of course," Mr. Hero said, as if it expected that to be the case.

With a sense that things were suddenly moving very quickly, Daphne let Mr. Hero inside. Of course, she would need to explain Mr. Hero to her dad, but she'd take care of that in the morning. Another problem bothered her, though.

"I can't go around calling you Mr. Hero. It would be too embarrassing." She pondered for a moment. "I'll call you Blubb because you're sort of a rubbery blob. If anybody asks, I'll tell them Blubb is short for Robert."

Mr. Hero was agreeable. He hopped up the stairs and followed her into her room.

"Do you sleep?" she asked Blubb.

"I can," Blubb said. He closed his eyes but continued to stand at the foot of her bed.

Having a large purple duck stand at the foot of her bed all night seemed ridiculous. "Can you do any shapes I haven't seen yet?" Daphne asked.

"I can do a lot of shapes," Blubb said eagerly.

He flowed until he assumed a form that so astonished Daphne she had to sit down hard on her bed. "You look like me, but smaller!" she cried. The form even wore the same jeans and *Star Trek* T-shirt that she was wearing. The left tennis shoe even had a stain where she had dripped some spaghetti sauce.

"Yes," Blubb said in Daphne's voice. "You're my friend. I want to look like you."

"But you're purple," Daphne said. And indeed, everything about Blubb had a purple cast, even the clothes.

"Is there something wrong with purple?" Blubb asked fearfully.

"No, no. It's just sort of"—Daphne searched for a word—"it's sort of unnatural."

Slowly Blubb's skin color changed to match Daphne's pale complexion.

"Very nice," Daphne said. Blubb was still faintly purple, but so light that no one would really notice.

Daphne walked around Blubb. It was eerie, like walking around a statue of herself, except that the statue breathed and fidgeted. She was a little pudgy, her nose was too big, and her eyes were too small. Still, her hair was clean and reasonably well combed.

Daphne finally decided that going around with a short twin would be too weird.

"Can you do boys?" Daphne asked.

"Only Sidney Agenda and Lowell Gravenstien in a ninja suit."

Daphne laughed. She was talking to herself! She decided that Blubb should specialize in boys after he gathered more samples. That way he would have less chance of doing her again. Apparently, she was already thinking of Blubb as a he. Well, he had started as *Mr.* Hero.

"Actually," Daphne said, "I liked you better as a cat. A cat is a good basic shape for a hero. A cat is also comfy to sleep with."

Blubb melted back into his cat shape, then curled up on the floor with his tail over his nose. "Is this all right?" he asked.

"Perfect," Daphne said. She lay in bed for a while, unable to sleep because she was too excited imagining how surprised Harv would be to hear about Lowell Gravenstien and see Blubb. She was still going over her plan to save Sidney Agenda when she drifted off to sleep.

The next morning Daphne was awakened by the electronic beeping of her Supertech handheld video game. She crawled to the end of her bed and was surprised to see Blubb sitting on the floor delicately punching the buttons with the human fingers of a human hand. The hand looked bizarre on the end of a cat arm.

"You play Supertech?" Daphne asked, amused.

"I guess I do," Blubb admitted. "I didn't know I knew."

"How did you learn, then?"

Blubb didn't know. As they talked Daphne discovered that he'd spent the night resting on top of the game.

"Could you have absorbed the knowledge through your skin?" Daphne asked. It seemed odd, but Blubb was odd.

To find out, they tried an experiment with the portable radio she sometimes wore clipped to her belt. She put it on the floor and asked him to sit on it. Instead, he put out a paw and

let it melt around the radio, covering it like grape gelatin. She was afraid the radio would be ruined, but when Blubb pulled back his paw, the radio was fine.

"Can you show me how it works?" she asked.

"Yes," Blubb said. He switched it on without a moment's hesitation.

Daphne was impressed. She was even more surprised when he took on the shape of her radio. Of course, she could still tell them apart—Blubb was much bigger.

"Can you sound like a radio, too?" Daphne asked.

"No. I know how to operate it, and I can look like it, but I can't *be* it."

That seemed like a defect in his design, Daphne decided. But she knew that the skills Blubb did have would come in handy when they raided Moe Prep. She went downstairs with him—a cat again—and found that her father had already left for work. If he'd looked in on her before he went—which was likely—or when he got home the night before, he obviously hadn't seen Blubb.

While Daphne ate cold cereal and milk for breakfast, she had Blubb absorb stuff around the house. He did the telephone, the television, and the VCR, and soon it occurred to her that she was missing a good bet. She put down her spoon.

Blubb followed her into the living room where she studied the boxes of books. She searched through them until she found the one she wanted. "See what you get out of this," she said, tossing him a hardcover with the title *Great Spy Stories.*

Blubb allowed the book to strike his body. It stuck, then it slowly sank in. He stood still for a moment, and then stepped away, leaving the book on the floor.

"Did you learn anything?"

" 'Rule Number One: A spy is inconspicuous.' " He backed against the wall and melted into the form of an armchair just like one that already stood in the room. Only the fact that Blubb still had a faint purplish cast allowed Daphne to tell them apart.

Daphne couldn't help smiling. "Pretty good," she said.

She let him absorb *The Complete Sherlock Holmes,* an atlas, an unabridged dictionary, and each volume of the encyclopedia. While she finished her breakfast, Blubb browsed among the rest of the books, going wherever his curiosity took him. *This is going to be great,* Daphne thought. As she discovered more and more about Blubb, she grew more hopeful about rescuing Sidney.

As she was washing up, someone knocked on the back door. It was Harv.

"Are you ready to save Sidney?" he asked.

Daphne said, "Come on in. I have something to show you."

When they got to the living room, Daphne pointed to the slightly purple cat washing its paws in the middle of the room. "This is Blubb," she said proudly. "Alias, Mr. Hero."

Harv's jaw dropped. Daphne explained what had happened the night before and what she'd discovered that morning. Blubb showed off his talents by popping a city atlas out of his mouth and catching it in one paw.

"I guess we're ready to storm Moe Prep," Harv said finally.

"Correction: We would be if we knew where it was," Daphne said.

"I thought you had a plan," Harv said.

"The plan is to find Moe Prep and rescue Sidney," Daphne reminded him, realizing as she said it how lame that sounded. "Maybe we can find a clue in the backyard. Lowell Gravenstien was crashing around down there before he attacked me."

"We could sure use a clue," Harv agreed.

NINE

Dress for Success

The three of them went outside to search. Blubb showed them the spot where he'd oozed partway under the hedge to observe the cats. But he couldn't help with Lowell Gravenstien. Blubb hadn't seen Lowell until he'd attacked Daphne.

Depressed, Daphne stood on one foot in the middle of the yard, picking leaves off the bottom of her raised shoe and watching Harv as he thrashed around in the undergrowth. The morning dew made everything damp and sticky.

Daphne pulled a gray slip of paper from the bottom of one foot. "What's this?" she asked. Harv ran over to see.

"It's a bus transfer," he said as they studied it.

"What's a bus?" Blubb asked. "And why would you want to transfer it?"

Harv took a few minutes to explain buses and transfers to Blubb.

Harv took the transfer from Daphne. "According to the way it's punched, it was from late yesterday."

"How do you know?" Daphne asked, a little surprised.

"I've been riding the bus for years. You pick up stuff."

"What line is it a transfer from?"

Harv pointed to the number that had been punched out. "Line sixty-three."

"Where does it go?"

"I'm not *that* good," Harv admitted. "But I have a stack of bus schedules at home. I *think* I have Line sixty-three."

Daphne felt a growing excitement. The transfer was a better clue than she'd first thought. Harv wasn't so sure, though. "This transfer might not mean anything," he said. "It could have blown in here from the street."

"Or, Lowell Gravenstien *might* have dropped it," Daphne said. "Anyway, it's the only clue we have."

Harv had to agree. He ran back to his house to get his schedules. As Daphne paced up and down the yard, Blubb ran, jumped, skipped, and hopped behind her in cat form.

"Stop that!" Daphne cried. "You're driving me crazy."

Blubb sat down under a tree and looked at

her with big solemn eyes. He was so cute that Daphne couldn't stay angry at him. She scratched him behind the ears and found to her astonishment that his fur actually felt like fur. "Okay," she said. "You can follow me. Just not so close."

Blubb nodded, but he watched from under the tree when Daphne began to pace again.

Harv brought back a thick stack of bus schedules and stared at them sadly.

"Don't worry," Daphne said. "Blubb can help us go through them."

Daphne put the bus schedules on the ground. Blubb melted one paw over the stack. A moment later he pulled his paw back and began to lick it, claws spread, as if he were a real cat.

"Where does Line sixty-three go, Blubb?" Daphne asked.

Blubb stopped washing and yawned. "Line sixty-three starts at the corner of Greenbean Avenue and Pineapple Street," he said, "and it goes up into the hills." Daphne noticed that his voice was gradually becoming less like hers. That was a relief anyway.

Harv considered the new information. "Moe Prep could be in the hills," he said. "It could be hidden up there."

"We'll have to check," Daphne said, "but

first we're going to have to change our clothes."

"Why?" Harv asked.

Daphne said, "Moe Prep is classy, and we're going to have to look classy to fit in."

"I hate wearing a tie," Harv said.

"I don't blame you," Daphne said. "But if I can wear the dress my aunt Anne gave me, you can wear a tie."

Harv went home to change. While Daphne did the same, Blubb settled down in the living room with Daphne's Supertech game.

Daphne poked through her closet and decided that Aunt Anne's dress was too fancy. Instead, she chose the sort of dress a parent might want her to wear on the first day of school. The blouse had some lace at the collar, which ought to do for Moe Prep.

Downstairs, she found Harv and Blubb waiting. Harv wore a gray suit and a blue clip-on tie, which he said he hadn't worn since his parents' wedding anniversary party some months before. Blubb was still in the shape of a cat.

"You can't go that way," Daphne said.

"Maybe he shouldn't go at all," Harv suggested.

"Why?" Daphne asked.

"If Blubb is what they're looking for, it

doesn't make sense to take him into the enemy's camp."

Daphne said, "I don't think anybody besides Sidney and us would know Mr. Hero outside of his jar. Lowell didn't. Besides, before we're done we may need a professional hero."

Harv agreed. "Makes sense to me."

"All right, Blubb," Daphne said. "Do your stuff."

Blubb flowed until he became a red-faced kid a full head shorter than Harv, complete with a tuxedo that was more purple than black. "I copied him from the encyclopedia," Blubb explained.

While they walked to the bus stop, Daphne kept glancing at Blubb, pleased and amazed at his disguise. Though he looked like a kid only a couple of years younger than they were, he trotted along like a two-year-old. Apparently Blubb couldn't learn everything instantly.

Following Blubb's directions, they took the Number fourteen bus, which dropped them at the corner of Greenbean Avenue and Pineapple Street.

The next bus took them up into the hills. Even if they had not been going to save somebody, riding the bus would have been exciting. Through the trees and brush, Daphne could look down for the first time onto the city. It was even larger than she had imagined. In all directions it spread to a misty horizon, except to the west, where it was stopped by the big gray ocean.

There were three other kid passengers, all well dressed; they weren't doing anything special, but Daphne thought dressing up in the summer was pretty weird and reason enough to be suspicious for her. They were uniformly serious and spoke in low whispers or scribbled in small notebooks. One had a portable computer that beeped and booped. She decided they had to be going to a summer school and hoped it was Moe Prep.

When the three kids got off together, Daphne, Harv, and Blubb followed them. They went up a steep hill through a beautiful forest.

The kids stopped in a small clearing among the trees. Daphne couldn't imagine why. She glanced at Harv, but he shrugged.

Then Daphne heard what she thought was thunder. A door in the hillside, paneled in rock and overgrown with bushes, slowly swung outward. The three kids calmly filed inside.

"Well?" Daphne asked.

"We might not be able to get out," Harv said.

"Why did we bother to come this far if we're not going in?" She almost hoped that Harv would have a good excuse why they shouldn't.

The thought of being buried alive inside that mountain was not nice.

Still moving like a two-year-old, Blubb trotted toward the vast open doorway which was already starting to close.

Feeling a deep dread, Daphne followed—Harv beside her.

TEN

The Lair of Evil Geniuses

They entered a large tunnel that smelled damp and turned all sound into ghostly echoes. As they walked, Daphne noticed glowing patches on the walls. Farther along the patches jutted out like teeth, and Daphne could see that they were crystals. She wondered if these crystals did more than just give off light. As they walked, the crystals became larger and closer together and some, almost as tall as she was, grew out of the tunnel floor.

At last they came to an enormous cavern so big that, for a moment, Daphne thought they'd walked all the way through the mountain and come out on the other side. But the ceiling of the cavern still arched hundreds of feet over them. The crystals spread out from the tunnel up to the ceiling. From the far end of the cavern, light entered through big windows that overlooked the city.

Then she noticed all the kids and adults in suits walking among well-tended beds of beautiful flowers. At the far end of the garden, near the windows, stood a square building with three domes. The dome in the middle was larger than the other two.

"This isn't what I expected," Harv said.

Daphne agreed with him. It was more like the grounds of a museum than the lair of evil geniuses. The only thing strange about it was that it was hidden inside a mountain. Was that any worse than being hidden behind an ice-cream shop, though? Daphne wanted to believe they were in no more danger than they had been at Paladin Tech, but she'd seen Lowell Gravenstien at work. The memory made her anxious.

"Do you have a plan," Harv asked, "or did I miss something?"

"Act casual," Daphne advised.

"A spy is inconspicuous," Blubb reminded them.

Harv nodded. He seemed uncomfortable.

Daphne was uncomfortable, too, because she had no idea what to do. She didn't know where to look for Sidney.

Despite the beautiful gardens, it was easy for Daphne to figure out something was wrong. Some adults wore suits, but when she looked closer, she noticed the odd costumes of the others. One wore a lab coat buttoned up to his chin and black rubber gloves that reached to his elbows—certainly hot and uncomfortable even inside an air-conditioned chamber. Another wore a cape with a huge batwing collar painted with lightning bolts.

Daphne actually felt better seeing people she could positively identify as evil.

As the three of them wandered around, Daphne saw that she'd been wrong about the grounds, too. They were considerably more sinister than they appeared at first glance.

They passed a water fountain, and Daphne was suddenly thirsty. It had been a long morning. "I need a drink," she said. She bent down to turn on the water and a few drops spattered her hand. "Yow!" she cried and jumped back. She tripped over a nearby bench, which shocked her with electricity. She stood on the path quivering, afraid to move.

"What?" Harv asked.

Breathing deeply, Daphne got a grip on herself. She was dealing with professional evil geniuses, and the three of them had better start acting like professional heroes or they were doomed. She pulled a scrap of paper from her pocket and allowed some of the liquid from the drinking fountain to run over it. Wherever the liquid touched, the paper hissed and dissolved.

"Acid," Harv said.

"Yeah," Daphne said. "What kind of people would put acid in their own water fountains?"

"Bad people," Blubb said.

"And don't sit on the benches. They're electrified."

Harv glanced around. "I see people sitting down."

"I guess they know how," Daphne said.

Harv nodded. His eyes never stopped moving. Daphne understood perfectly. If the drinking fountains were full of acid, and the benches were electrified, what other surprises were waiting for them?

"What's that?" Harv asked, pointing to a cube on a pedestal. It was a few feet on a side, and seemed to be made of crushed metal.

Blubb stepped forward and read in a singsong voice, " 'Encased here in his own Lincoln Continental are the mortal remains of Wilfred Teaberry. Let this be a warning to any who would compete with the James Moriarty Preparatory School for Young Gentlemen and Ladies.' What does that mean?"

Daphne squirmed as she imagined what it was like to be crushed inside your own car.

"It means, my friend," a voice behind them said, "that Mr. Teaberry tried to start his own school for evil geniuses."

Surprised, they turned and saw Lowell Gravenstien and two of his friends, each casually paddling a rubber ball. The balls were attached to the paddles by rubber bands. Daphne briefly admired them. She had never been able to get the hang of those paddleballs.

"Surely it's Sidney Agenda's two friends," Lowell said with delight. "I'm afraid I don't know this third gentleman." He nodded at Blubb.

"Another friend," Daphne said. She could see why pencil-counting Aunt Millicent approved of Lowell. He was so polite, he made Daphne's teeth hurt.

"Of course he is," Lowell said. "Please come with us."

"No thanks," Daphne said. "We're just visiting." She hoped that she sounded more self-assured than she felt.

"I'm afraid I must insist," Lowell said.

Before Daphne had a chance to move, he suddenly paddled the rubber ball at her. It swung around her, wrapping her arms tightly against her body with the rubber band. The rubber band was thick and strong and couldn't be snapped. The other two boys shot their balls, and Harv and Blubb found themselves tied up, too.

"You won't get away with this," Daphne said, though she knew they were empty words.

She wished she'd had at least one class at Paladin Tech. Knowing a little something about the hero business would have been helpful. "We're the good guys!"

"That is your problem, I'm afraid," Lowell said. "Come along." He and his two friends pulled them toward the big building. Daphne tried to keep her spirits up, but she couldn't help being terrified. Was it better or worse to be caught by an evil genius who was still a student of his craft? Would he be more merciful or less?

In the center of the garden was a round pond. A bridge led to a cement island complete with a fake plastic palm tree. A sign near the bridge said PIRANHA POOL.

The sign dismayed Daphne. Piranhas were tiny fish that, in the movies at least, could eat a person in seconds.

"Are there really piranhas in there?" she asked.

"Of course," Lowell Gravenstien said. "The daily feeding of the piranhas at sundown is quite lovely. The bridge is made to collapse, and in the food goes, *ker-splash!*" He shook his head. "It would be a pity for you to miss it, but at sundown you and your friends may still be all tied up."

Blubb took in this information as casually as

he took in any other, but Daphne and Harv shared a worried glance. She wondered who that evening's guest of honor would be.

The big building had brass doors, with sharp metal studs poking out of them. Inside, the air was cool. They walked down a long hallway with classrooms on either side. Many seemed to have classes going on. In one, a woman dressed like a witch was leading her class in cackling exercises. Daphne couldn't help but stare as they passed.

Finally Lowell and his friends stopped and straightened their ties. "Try not to embarrass me," Lowell requested, and he pushed Daphne, Harv, and Blubb into the next room.

They found themselves face to face with a pirate wearing a bandanna, a single gold ring in one ear, and knee-length britches. He wore a leather vest over his bare chest and no shoes. On one cheek was a jagged scar. He looked so much like the pirates Daphne had seen in movies, she didn't know whether to laugh or cry.

"Where's his parrot?" Harv whispered.

"Avast there!" the pirate cried. "By thunder, the prisoners'll not speak till they're spoke to." He turned to Lowell. "You be late," he grumbled.

"I'm sorry, Mr. Humble-Bellows," Lowell said. "I was just picking up my show-and-tell exhibit."

Mr. Humble-Bellows nodded. "Show-and-tell, is it? You be a first-class gentleman, Mr. Gravenstien. Let's see this here exhibit."

"Yes, sir," Lowell said.

Daphne took a quick glance around the classroom. The students were not dressed like pirates, but wore suits like Lowell and his friends.

"All quiet, says I!" Mr. Humble-Bellows cried.

Lowell paced while his friends brought three chairs and pushed Daphne, Harv, and Blubb into them. Their arms were still bound by the rubber bands of the paddleballs.

"What shall we talk about?" Lowell asked in a tone that managed to be pleasant and sinister at once. It made Daphne shiver. When none of them answered, he continued. "I have some questions for you. If you answer them promptly and properly, it will go easier for all of us."

Mr. Humble-Bellows sat down at a desk in the back of the room and began to make marks on a clipboard.

No one said anything. Lowell seemed to have expected this. "Where is Mr. Hero?" he asked.

Daphne was afraid that Blubb would speak up, but evidently he'd been designed well enough to keep secrets from bad guys.

"Mister *what?*" Daphne asked. If they tortured her, she might end up telling everything she knew, but she didn't want to make it too easy.

"Come, come, now. You were with Sidney Agenda when we found him. Later, when we captured him, he no longer had his jar of Mr. Hero. If you don't have the jar, you must have given it to somebody else."

"How is Sidney?" Harv asked politely.

"Enough talk," Mr. Humble-Bellows called from the back of the room. "Time to be using more convincing measures."

Lowell seemed nervous. "I was just warming up," he assured Mr. Humble-Bellows.

"The tides won't wait," Mr. Humble-Bellows said.

Lowell turned back to his captives. "You force me to a terrible decision," he said.

Daphne's mind instantly thought up a number of horrifying possibilities.

"Class dismissed," Mr. Humble-Bellows said. "Mr. Gravenstien and I'll be having a little private chat with the prisoners."

Under Mr. Humble-Bellows's critical eye, Lowell prodded Daphne, Harv, and Blubb to their feet and out the door.

"Where are we going?" Harv asked.

"To the shower room," Lowell said. "We'll see if a little freezing cold water will change your minds about cooperating."

"I take cold showers all the time," Daphne claimed, though it wasn't true. She had been forced to take a cold shower once at summer camp and hated it.

"We'll see," Lowell said with an evil smirk.

ELEVEN

All Reefs and Typhoons

As they marched down the hallway—Lowell in the lead, Mr. Humble-Bellows bringing up the rear—a gong rang and the hallway began to fill with students.

Suddenly Blubb broke free and in seconds vanished into the growing crowd.

"Go, Blubb!" Daphne and Harv cried.

"Avast there!" Mr. Humble-Bellows cried. "Catch him! Catch him or it'll go rum for the likes of you, by thunder!"

Lowell ran into the crowd, thrusting kids out of the way as he went. Mr. Humble-Bellows grabbed Daphne and Harv by the arms and growled at them.

Lowell made a search of the hallway and all the rooms that lined it. He stopped occasionally to spin a kid around, but it was never Blubb. As time went on and Lowell continued to come up empty-handed, Daphne's spirits rose. With Blubb free they might all have a chance of being rescued.

The next period started, and once more the hallway emptied. Lowell marched up to Daphne and Harv and glared.

"My grades have been perfect till now," Lowell said. "I don't intend to allow amateurs such as yourselves to lower my grade-point average."

"Sidney told us you had a good chance of taking over the world," Harv said. "I guess he was wrong."

Daphne couldn't help laughing.

Lowell grew even angrier. He roughly pushed Harv and Daphne down the hall.

Daphne had no intention of attempting to escape, not at the moment, anyway. Escaping had been easy enough for Blubb: She imagined that once he'd broken free, he'd turned himself into a potted palm or a piece of furniture or even into some other kid he'd seen—some shape that would allow him to easily wriggle out of his rubber-band bonds. But she and Harv were stuck looking like themselves.

"What kind of a name is Blubb, anyway?" Lowell spat out.

"It's short for Robert," Daphne explained offhandedly.

"Whatever be his name," Mr. Humble-Bellows said from behind them, "I don't call him proud, leaving his friends behind like this."

"My grade—" Lowell began.

"Aye," Mr. Humble-Bellows said. "You be smart as paint, but as for luck, it be all reefs and typhoons. Shove along, Mr. Gravenstien, shove along."

They passed the Reichenbach Gymnasium and waited outside the boys' locker room while Lowell went to make sure no one was using it. Mr. Humble-Bellows gripped each of them tighter.

Lowell came out and reported the locker room and showers were empty. He hung a CLOSED sign on the door and hurried Daphne and Harv inside. Mr. Humble-Bellows followed.

They passed hundreds of lockers and came to a tiled room that had shower nozzles on each side. Mr. Humble-Bellows took up a position near the entrance of the room. From there, he paid close attention to everything that happened and made an occasional mark on his clipboard with a pencil.

"It's such a pity to see your nice clothes ruined," Lowell said as though he meant it. "You can save us all a lot of trouble by telling me where Mr. Hero is."

"I have other clothes," Harv said.

"Me, too," Daphne said, glad that she had not worn the party dress after all.

"Very well," Lowell said. He shoved them under a nozzle and, with a flourish, twisted the cold-water knob.

Daphne steeled herself for the cold shower, but the pipe above her only gurgled for a few seconds. No water came out.

Lowell glanced at Mr. Humble-Bellows, but Mr. Humble-Bellows just stared blankly.

"I'll give you another chance," Lowell said.

When neither Daphne nor Harv said anything, he pulled them under another nozzle and again tried the cold water. This time he didn't even get a gurgle.

Daphne wondered what was going on. One shower might be out of order, but two in a row was more lucky coincidence than she and Harv had any right to expect. It might be Blubb, but Daphne had no idea how he could be helping them.

"Your last chance!" Lowell cried. Without waiting for an answer, he pulled them under another shower and twisted the knob. A furious banging came, but no water.

Frowning, Lowell joined Mr. Humble-Bellows by the exit for a conference. Daphne looked around for another way out. The room had windows, but they were all near the ceiling and covered with metal mesh.

Suddenly a hard shower of water sprayed

down at Lowell and Mr. Humble-Bellows from the nozzle nearest to them. Mr. Humble-Bellows dropped his clipboard as he and Lowell yelled and ran.

Daphne and Harv saw their chance. They darted out into the locker room before Lowell and Mr. Humble-Bellows could chase them.

"Where to?" Harv asked.

"The tunnel," Daphne said.

Running with her hands tied against her sides proved difficult. Harv waddled along beside her like a penguin, but neither of them had a choice.

They pounded down the paths between the flower beds and entered the tunnel. Many of the crystals stood five or six feet tall. They were as big around as trees, and had sharp edges against which the kids sawed their rubber-band restraints. In a moment the bands snapped with loud *sproings*.

Harv collected the cut rubber bands, and the two of them ducked behind a wall of crystals, and waited behind it, trembling. Any moment now Daphne expected hundreds of students to pour from the building, each armed with a paddleball paddle. She wondered why she and Harv even bothered to hide.

But life on campus continued normally. Students and teachers continued to stroll to their classes, seemingly without a care.

"Can you beat that?" Daphne commented.

"You know, if we're Lowell's class project," Harv suggested, "and he's the only one who's interested in us, maybe we shouldn't expect to be chased by anyone but him. I mean, if a white mouse escaped from your classroom, would you alert the entire school?"

"Probably not," Daphne admitted. "Still, he'll probably come after us eventually."

Harv nodded. They heard someone coming and were about to duck behind the crystals again until they saw who it was.

"Blubb!" Daphne cried.

"You made it, dude," Harv said. "We almost didn't get away. Our luck was incredible."

"It wasn't luck," Blubb said proudly. "It was me. I untangled myself—"

"How?" Daphne asked.

"Like this," Blubb said. He grew an arm from the top of his head and made unwrapping motions with the hand at the end of it. "I just unwrapped myself."

"Wow," Harv said.

Daphne nodded. Blubb hadn't used the method she'd thought of, but it impressed her just the same. "How did you do the showers?" she asked.

"Guess," Blubb said and laughed.

Daphne and Harv were surprised by Blubb's response Apparently, Blubb had the social skills of a three-year-old. But, that was actually pretty impressive. It would take a *real* kid three years to act like a three-year-old.

"We don't have time to guess," Daphne explained as gently as she could. She looked out through the tunnel entrance. "Lowell Gravenstien is after us."

"Oh." Blubb acted pouty for a moment. "Okay," he said at last. "I knew Lowell was going to make you take cold showers, but I didn't know where the shower room was, so after I escaped I made myself real thin and went into the pipes through a garden hose."

"A tight fit!" Daphne exclaimed.

"Tighter than the jar," Blubb agreed. "But the most fun was when I let all the water out onto Lowell and Mr. Humble-Bellows."

They all had a good laugh over that.

"How did you find the right shower?" Harv asked.

"It's easy," Blubb said. "I broke up into pieces and I—"

"You what?" Harv exclaimed.

"I broke up into pieces and I sent them all over the water system and—"

"Through all the pipes?" Daphne asked.

"Uh-huh," Blubb said.

"Blubbettes," Daphne said, amazed. Apparently Blubb had talents none of them expected. If what he said was true, he could divide himself into pieces and send each piece on a mission. Sidney Agenda became more worth saving all the time.

Blubb liked the word. He said *Blubbettes* over and over.

Daphne said, "This is serious, Blubb. We're in trouble."

"Oh," Blubb said.

"What did you do after you went through all the pipes?" Harv asked.

"Well," Blubb said, "before I stuffed up the showers I found a lot of neat stuff. I found bathrooms, and I found a river, and I found the sprinklers—"

"A river?" Daphne asked excitedly. "Where?"

"Underground," Blubb said.

"Bingo," Harv said.

"You think it's the Thames?" Daphne asked him.

"If the Thames can run under your house, it can run under Moe Prep." He shrugged. "Besides, how many rivers could there be under this city? Right?"

"Right," Daphne and Blubb said together.

"Can you take us there?" Daphne asked.

"Sure," Blubb said and strode off.

"Not now," Daphne said, calling him back. "We have to find Sidney first."

"I can find him," Blubb said, pleased.

Daphne was astonished. "Since when?" she asked.

"Since I heard Lowell and his teacher talk after I squirted them," Blubb said.

"Well, where is he?" Daphne asked impatiently.

"Lowell said he was keeping Sidney in the Reichenbach Gym."

"A location is still not a plan," Harv said.

"I could distract Lowell," Blubb offered.

"You could?" Daphne asked.

"Sure. Sidney Agenda gave me distracting skills." He smiled.

Daphne glanced at Harv. Harv shrugged. She decided to give Blubb a chance. If he was the perfect artificial hero, it made sense.

The three of them walked to the end of the tunnel and looked around the campus of Moe Prep. It seemed quiet. Then Daphne pointed out Lowell walking among the flower beds with his hands shoved deep into his pockets. He looked angry. Now and then he stopped to peer into a trash can.

"If he thinks I'd hide in a trash can," Daphne said, "he doesn't know me at all."

Blubb allowed himself to melt into a long narrow shape, something like a skinny rat, including teeth, ears, and a tail. Daphne and Harv backed away from him, their eyes wide.

"I'm the Giant Rat of Sumatra," Blubb explained. "From a Sherlock Holmes story."

"That should distract him," Harv said.

"Scary," Daphne agreed. "How come you're pink?"

"Sumatra was that color in the atlas."

Daphne nodded. That would make sense to a three-year-old. "Can you do black?" she asked. "A darker color would be scarier."

Blubb closed his eyes and scrunched up his mouth. Slowly he turned black with a purple cast. "This is my darkest," he said.

Daphne gulped. She didn't mind small white laboratory rats, but she really hated the big black kind that lived under houses and in sewers. Blubb the rat had a nasty look to him. Daphne was horrified, even though she knew this creature was really her pal.

"Good enough," she said, swallowing. "Go distract him."

"I'll distract him good," Blubb said. He dashed forward, taking short runs this way and that. At last he honed in on Lowell.

When Lowell saw Blubb coming, he turned and ran with a shriek of fear.

"Let's do it," Daphne said. They headed for the gymnasium.

TWELVE

Acting the Part

The gym was a high, long room with a polished wooden floor. At the far end barefoot students were flinging themselves around on mats. Each wore what looked like white pajamas.

Their instructor was a short thick man wearing a bowler hat and a shiny suit about a size too small for him. He communicated by waving his hands and making faces.

Opposite Daphne and Harv, ropes hung from the ceiling by hooks. The last hook and rope supported a cage a good ten feet off the ground. Inside the cage sat Sidney Agenda, his feet dangling between the bars and a gag in his mouth. Sidney's eyes widened when he saw them.

"Now what?" Harv asked.

Daphne saw no easy solution. To get Sidney down, they would have to cross a big open space, untie the rope from the cleat in the wall, and lower Sidney to the floor. They would then have to get the cage open and walk out of the gym with him. She reckoned they had no chance.

"We could climb the outside of the building to the roof," she said, "and come down through a hole in the ceiling." But she knew it was a bad idea even before Harv shook his head.

"Hey, Daf, we look as if we belong here," Harv said. "Maybe we should act like it for a change."

Harv's idea made sense. Nobody had paid any attention to them in the hallway, and nobody was looking at them now.

Before Daphne could have second thoughts, Harv began to walk across the gym as if he owned it. Daphne caught up and walked next to him. Sidney seemed to be miles away.

A single loud clap stopped them. Daphne and Harv saw the instructor and his students looking at them. The instructor smiled in an unpleasant way.

One of the students bowed. "Master Ojo says that you are late," the student said. "He asks that you join us."

"We're a little busy at the moment," Daphne said.

"He asks that you join us *now,*" the student said.

Master Ojo smiled again.

"What do we do?" Daphne whispered to Harv.

Harv shrugged. "Join them," he said. Daphne

glanced up at Sidney, who was calmly watching everything that happened.

Daphne and Harv walked to the line of students at the very back of the class. Harv looked as worried as Daphne felt. She had seen any number of spy movies, and she'd goofed around with her friends, but when it came to real martial arts she knew absolutely nothing. She was sure that would become obvious the moment they started. If they were lucky, this would be a beginner class.

"*Taikyoku* number one!" the student helper cried out. Everyone copied the instructor's stance—with their feet spread and their fists floating at their sides. The instructor moved gracefully from one pose to another, punching with a fist, kicking with a leg. Daphne followed as best she could. It would have been fun if she hadn't been so scared.

She didn't know how long she and Harv were doing *Taikyoku* number one before a door to the gym banged open. Daphne, who was already fidgety, jumped. The instructor and his students stopped doing their exercise and stared.

Lowell Gravenstien rolled what looked like a big silver barrel into the gym. He seemed angry and determined. "Resistance is useless!" he screamed at Harv and Daphne. What had happened to Blubb?

"Come on," Harv said. He and Daphne ran to the cleat where the rope holding Sidney's cage was tied. "Distract 'em," Harv said. He pulled out a pocket knife and sawed at the rope.

Daphne licked her lips and moved away from Harv without an idea in her head. Lowell Gravenstien was busy with his silver barrel. Apparently Harv's white mouse theory was correct, because nobody else seemed interested in what they were doing now that it was clear they were not really part of the class.

"Hang on!" Harv cried.

Daphne turned as the last few strands of the rope unraveled. The cage crashed to the floor, denting the hard wood. Harv reached between the bars and removed Sidney's gag. "Are you okay?" he asked.

"Yeah, I'm fine. One of the first things a hero learns is how to fall."

"Well, *I'm* impressed," Harv said.

"Yo, Gravenstien!" Sidney cried out. "You still using that old trick?"

"What trick is that?" Daphne asked.

"The Walking Springs," Sidney whispered out the side of his mouth. "If one gets near you, it's curtains."

Daphne soon understood Sidney's strange remark. When Lowell stood the barrel up and pushed it over, she could see that it wasn't a barrel at all, but a big spring, a giant Slinky. The top arched over and touched the floor. Then what had been the bottom sprang up so that *it* became the top. The new top then flipped onto the floor. In this way, end over end, the big spring made a soft whirring sound as it headed toward them.

"Resistance is useless," Lowell said again.

As the big spring flipped closer, Daphne and Harv stepped away from Sidney, and for a moment, the spring hesitated. Then, to Daphne's horror, it broke apart into three smaller springs. One of the springs came after each of them.

The spring chasing Sidney leaped at him, but could no more get into the cage than Sidney could get out. "Nyah, nyah!" Sidney cried and stuck out his tongue at the spring.

Suddenly the spring chasing Daphne flung itself at her. She was momentarily startled, which was long enough for the top of the spring to slip down over her. She was imprisoned inside a silver cylinder. She tried desperately to push the thing over.

"Resistance is— ulp!" she heard Lowell say. Lowell obviously had a problem. That was all right with Daphne. Suddenly something *whooshed* by her.

"Wait!" Lowell cried. "Stop! You can't!"

A space appeared between the bottom of the spring and the floor, and Daphne slid through it. Sidney and Harv had been holding the spring up, and now they dropped it with a grunt. How had Sidney gotten out of his cage?

Then Daphne spotted Blubb, back in his kid form.

"Let's blow this Popsicle stand!" Sidney cried. They all ran for the door. They made it outside and hid behind a hedge to plan.

"Where now?" Harv asked.

Sidney said, "Look."

Lowell was coming out of the building. He must have convinced the karate class to help because he was followed by the entire group. They poured down the steps and spread out in the formal gardens. Mr. Humble-Bellows and the karate instructor observed from the front steps.

Daphne's heart sank. "They're sure to be watching the tunnel," she said. "Is there another way out?"

"There's always another way," Sidney assured her. "I just don't know where it is. Do you, Mr. Hero?"

Blubb shook his head, his eyes open wide.

Daphne was about to point out that an escape route that nobody could find was as useful as no escape route at all, when she recalled the conversation with Blubb in the tunnel.

"You said you knew where a river is, Blubb," she said.

"Yes," Blubb said, nodding.

"How do we get to it?" Daphne asked.

"Through the water pipes," Blubb said.

Daphne's hopes faded quickly.

Suddenly a small purple rat bounded up to them, leaped into the air, and merged into Blubb.

"I know another way to get to the river," Blubb said.

"That was a Blubbette, wasn't it, Blubb?" Daphne asked.

She immediately saw that she'd made a mistake by asking that question because Blubb began to repeat the word *Blubbette* over and over.

"Mr. Hero," Sidney said sternly.

Blubb stopped talking and stared at the ground while he stuck a finger up his nose.

Sidney threw an arm around Blubb's shoulders. "Could you lead us to the other way?"

"Oh," Blubb said, immediately brightening. "Okay."

They waited until nobody was looking, then ran for it. Daphne felt like a first-class target. She hoped that Blubb's "other way" wasn't far.

When they burst from behind the hedge a cry went up. In seconds Lowell Gravenstien and the karate class were after them, whooping like savages.

Blubb led them to a metal grating set in the middle of a grassy square of lawn. They lifted the heavy piece of metal and slid it to one side. Below was a stairway much like the one under Daphne's house. They hustled down the stairs, but hadn't gotten far when they heard Lowell's voice.

"They must have gone down here!" he cried.

Daphne looked around desperately, but saw no place to hide.

THIRTEEN

Double Agent

"Stand here," Sidney ordered. He pulled Daphne against the wall next to him and Harv. "Be the wall, Mr. Hero," he said.

To Daphne's surprise, Blubb spread over them like a thick coating of oil. It felt cool and smooth, and Blubb even left a little hollow in front of her face so she could breathe. She heard Lowell pound down the steps with the karate class in tow.

Daphne held her breath and realized that this was a trick that would never have occurred to her or to Blubb. Perhaps Sidney's training at Paladin Tech had paid off after all.

It seemed to take Lowell forever to search for them, and the air in Daphne's hollow became stale. She breathed shallowly, hoping to conserve oxygen. Finally she heard Lowell and his army march back up the stairs. The noise faded, and she heard the grating being slid back into place.

Blubb regained his kid form and danced

around clapping his hands. "We fooled 'em, we fooled 'em," he sang.

"We won't fool them long if you keep making that racket," Sidney said.

"Oh," Blubb said.

"You done good," Daphne said.

"You done *real* good," Harv said.

Blubb smiled.

They made their way down the rest of the stairs into the cool dampness, the smell of wet cement rising to meet them. Daphne could see why Lowell and the karate students had taken so long to search, for there were hundreds of stairs. They ended at a narrow river rushing between man-made cement banks. Its ripples glimmered under the electric lights set at intervals along the low ceiling. It ran a long way in each direction until it vanished around curves.

"Is it the Thames?" Daphne asked.

"It's just as much the Thames as the river under your house," Sidney said.

"That's no answer," Daphne said angrily. "Don't you trust us yet?"

"I trust you," Sidney said. "But it's not a matter of trust. It's a matter of faith."

"Faith in what?" Harv asked. "In us?"

"As in 'have faith,'" Sidney told them. "Come on, Mr. Hero." Turning, he walked along the bank with Blubb.

"I say we take him back to the gym," Daphne said hotly. Harv laughed at that.

Blubb jumped into the water and made whooping sounds at the cold. He stretched himself thin, forming a small raft with an oar on each side. Sidney climbed into the raft and sat down, making a little depression wherever he put his weight.

"Come on if you're coming," he said.

Even with just Sidney in it, the Blubb raft looked like it might sink. But unless she wanted to stay at Moe Prep forever, she would have to take her chances. Sighing, Daphne climbed into the raft across from Sidney. Harv came next, and with the three of them, it seemed *very* low in the water.

"How do you know which way to go?" Daphne asked.

"*I* don't know," Sidney said. "*Mr. Hero* knows. I designed him to have a homing instinct. I didn't know it was going to be *your* home." He shook his head. "Home, Mr. Hero."

Blubb paddled down the underground river. It thrilled Daphne to ride like that.

Now and then the river divided, but Blubb never hesitated. He knew exactly where to go.

After many minutes of silence Sidney suddenly spoke. "You guys had your nerve, opening my jar," he said.

Daphne gaped at him. Was this their thanks? "We didn't *have* to save you," she grumbled.

"Mr. Hero saved me—not you."

"How?" Daphne asked. "How did he open the cage?"

Sidney just smiled knowingly, which seemed ridiculous to Daphne. In fact, everything about Sidney struck her as ridiculous.

"He shoved his hand into the lock and popped it open," Harv said. "I guess he could feel around inside until his hand was the same shape as a key."

"I was going to tell her," Sidney said angrily.

Then Daphne became aware of a roar that had been getting louder for some time. "What's that?" she asked.

"Waterfall," Sidney said calmly.

"Down here?" Daphne exclaimed.

"We got water," Sidney said. "We got gravity. What's your problem?"

"I just— Oh!" The water surged faster, and she had to cling to the raft's sides to keep from spilling overboard. All three of them screamed as the raft went over a ledge and dumped them out.

As Daphne fell, water pounded on top of her. She fell for a long time, and then suddenly she realized she wasn't falling anymore. The roaring water did keep thrusting her under, but

when the water grew calmer, she naturally rose to the surface. Harv was already floating, and soon Sidney bobbed up beside them. Blubb drifted nearby in his raft form—all of them unharmed.

The three of them climbed back aboard Blubb and sat shivering as he rowed them down the river.

"Is it much farther?" Harv asked.

"Depends," Sidney said.

"He doesn't know," Daphne declared. She felt cold and miserable and blamed it all on Sidney.

Twenty minutes later Blubb docked at the bottom of a stone staircase. They climbed out and together pulled the Blubb raft ashore. He immediately turned into the kid again and was as drenched as they were.

"Let's do it again!" he cried. He wasn't even out of breath.

"Let's not and say we did," Harv replied.

They walked upstairs with Blubb in tow. "Blubbette, Blubbette," he repeated to himself.

When Harv pushed up the trapdoor, Daphne saw her house above them. They took Blubb into the downstairs bathroom. Sidney took one end of Blubb, and she and Harv took the other, and they wrung him out like a rag over the tub. "Yay! Yah!" Blubb cried in delight.

Daphne put on dry clothes while Harv ran home to change. She gave Sidney her dad's old flannel bathrobe and threw their wet clothes into the dryer.

Then they sat at the kitchen table and plotted over potato chips and soda.

"Don't you eat?" Harv asked Blubb.

"I guess not," Blubb said. The question did not concern him, which seemed odd because he was still in the form of the boy. In Daphne's experience, boys were always hungry.

"Mr. Hero isn't just your average everyday artificial creature," Sidney assured them. "He doesn't need to eat. He gets his energy the same way a plant does, from what you call photosynthesis."

"He makes energy out of sunlight?" Daphne asked, amazed.

"Yeah. Good idea, huh?" Sidney was obviously pleased with himself.

Apparently there were still many things to learn about Blubb, Daphne thought. "How did you keep Lowell away from us for so long?" she asked Blubb.

Blubb giggled. "He dropped the drawbridge over the piranha pool."

"Say what?" Sidney said, frowning.

"Oh. I chased him across the bridge and onto the island. He pulled a lever, and I fell into the piranha pool."

"That's must have been awful," Daphne said.

"No," Blubb explained. "I am one hundred percent artificial ingredients." The long words sounded odd in Blubb's mouth—as if he'd memorized them without knowing what they meant. "The piranhas only like real meat. They just took a sniff and swam away."

"So you climbed out," Harv prompted, "and walked away as somebody else."

Blubb nodded enthusiastically.

"What about Lowell?" Daphne asked.

Blubb smiled happily. "I broke the drawbridge off," he said, "So Lowell was stuck on the island surrounded by piranhas until somebody saved him."

Sidney chuckled. "What a guy you are, Mr. Hero!" he exclaimed.

"I'm Blubb now," Blubb said. "That's what Daphne calls me."

Sidney glanced at Daphne. "You got your nerve changing Mr. Hero's name."

"Do we have time for this now?" Harv asked. "We should be talking about Lowell."

Sidney thought about that for a moment. "All right," he said. "We'll talk about names later. Lowell won't give up easily."

"As far as I can see," Daphne said, "talking about how evil Lowell is isn't getting us anywhere. What I want to know is how he knew about the jar in the first place, and how he knew it was here." She knocked on the kitchen table.

"Hmm," Sidney said.

"Who knew about the jar?" Harv asked.

"I did, of course," Sidney said. "And Mr. Solo, my teacher. And Aunt Millicent, of course." He rolled his eyes at the ceiling, thinking who else might know.

Suddenly the whole conspiracy became clear to Daphne. "Your aunt Millicent is a double agent, Sidney. She must have told Lowell about the jar."

"That's it!" Harv cried.

Daphne and Harv looked at Sidney and waited for a verdict. Blubb began to kick his chair, but nobody bothered to tell him to stop.

"Sounds good," Sidney agreed. "Only thing is, you're wrong."

"Your aunt isn't a double agent?" Harv asked.

"Oh, Aunt Millicent may call Lowell with the occasional crumb, but not because she's a secret agent for Moe Prep. She's just a sucker for Lowell's good manners. Adults love that kind of thing."

Harv nodded. "Sure," he said. "If he was polite enough, she'd probably tell him anything he asked for."

"She didn't tell *us* anything," Daphne reminded him." And we were much more polite than she was."

"She was probably just cranky because we hadn't come to fix the copy machine," Harv said with a smile.

"You may be right," Daphne said. "But for whatever reason, your aunt Millicent is passing information on to the enemy."

"Good theory," Sidney said. "But who knows? Aunt Millicent might be innocent. Mr. Solo might have told. Or you or Harv might be a double agent."

Sidney's suggestion jolted Daphne.

When Sidney chuckled, Harv took a deep breath. "So what do we do?" he asked. "Point fingers at each other all afternoon?"

"Nope," Sidney said. "You got a phone?"

"It should have been connected this morning," Daphne said. "Why?"

Sidney smiled. "Watch and learn," he said.

Daphne hated to be treated like a spectator at a magic show, but she could see that Sidney had no intention of telling them anything more. Shaking her head, she showed him to the telephone and lifted the receiver to check for a dial tone.

Sidney called his aunt Millicent at Paladin Tech and told her that he and his jar of Mr. Hero were safe in their old house.

He listened for a moment and then said, "I will," before he hung up.

"Will what?" Harv asked.

"She reminded me to play nice," Sidney said.

Of course, Daphne thought. "Will you write down Paladin Tech's phone number?" she asked.

"Sure," Sidney said sarcastically. "I'll bet you want to know my blood type and my middle name, too."

"If Harv and I had had that number," Daphne said with scorn, "we could have saved you a lot sooner."

"If I can't trust my aunt Millicent," Sidney asked, "how can I trust you?"

"For one thing," Daphne said, "correct manners are not my life."

"For another," Harv said, "we're smarter than she is."

"I'm smarter than she is, too," Blubb said.

Sidney considered these facts. Without saying a word, he wrote down the number on a pad near the telephone. Daphne tore off the top sheet, and the three sheets below it, too. She'd seen enough mysteries on TV to know that a pen or pencil made an impression on the next few sheets, and those impressions could be read.

They went back to the kitchen to wait for something to happen. If Lowell didn't arrive, it might mean Aunt Millicent was innocent or that Lowell was too smart for them.

They sat for half an hour. Blubb amused them by changing from a boy to a small elephant and then to a lot of things he'd seen on the bus. Then all at once he quit and rested in a puddle in the sink.

"Maybe we were wrong," Daphne said. "Maybe—"

They heard a noise. First it was just a faraway hum. As it approached, it sounded more like hundreds of enormous birds whipping the air with their wings.

Blubb rose from the sink in his boy mode, and the four of them ran to look out the window.

A cloud of black specks filled half the sky. The cloud came from the direction of the hills, from the direction of the James Moriarty Preparatory School for Young Gentlemen and Ladies.

"Here they come," Blubb said unnecessarily.

FOURTEEN

One Ninja More or Less

"He wants a jar of purple stuff," Harv said. "I say we give him a jar of purple stuff."

"Not me!" Blubb cried with alarm.

"Chill out, dude," Sidney said. "We won't sacrifice you."

"I don't know whether we have anything in the house that's smooth enough and the right shade of purple," Daphne said. She glanced worriedly out the window. The flying things, whatever they were, were getting closer.

"Ice cream?" Harv suggested. "Bubble gum?"

"Haven't been shopping yet," Daphne said. "And I don't think I tried grape bubble gum more than once. It had sort of a chemical flavor."

The specks grew larger, and soon Daphne could see that each one was a person. Despite her fears, Daphne couldn't help laughing. Each of the flying people was wearing a propeller beanie. The propellers were what made the strange flapping noise, which got louder as they approached.

"Meowser brand cat food," she said suddenly.

"What about it?" Harv asked.

"You said you wanted to get rid of it. Here's your chance." When Daphne explained what she had in mind, Harv, Sidney, and Blubb agreed that it was a good idea, but it would take split-second timing and a lot of luck.

"A good plan today is better than a perfect plan tomorrow," Sidney said. "Let's get on it. Where are my clothes?"

Daphne got them from the dryer, and Sidney threw them on. Harv and Sidney hurried next door while Daphne found the box of garbage bags. Harv and Sidney returned carrying shopping bags full of Meowser brand cat food.

Daphne opened cans as fast as she could. When her hand got tired, Harv took a turn. As the cans were opened, Sidney spooned the contents into one of the bags. Soon the thick odors of cat tuna, cat beef, cat chicken, cat mixed grill, and cat ocean delight hung heavily in the kitchen.

"Disgusting, isn't it?" Harv noted.

The sound of the propeller beanies rattled the windows. Daphne imagined her house in the middle of its own private tornado. Everyone worked faster. She hoped they would have time to finish.

After they'd dumped the last of the cat food into the garbage bag, it was about a quarter full, and the kids could see out the window that Lowell Gravenstien's forces were circling the house. Their propellers made the gravelly thunder of lawn mower engines.

"Ninjas in propeller beanies," Harv said, amazed.

"I told you Lowell was one heavy dude," Sidney said grimly.

Daphne helped Harv and Sidney drag the garbage bag out to the backyard. The noise of the propeller beanies beat louder and louder, like the wings of attacking birds ready to swoop down. The flying ninjas fascinated her, but she didn't have time to watch them fly.

"Come on!" she said.

The nearest ninjas noticed them and began to circle lower.

Quickly Daphne encouraged Blubb to crawl into the garbage bag that Harv was holding open. The ninjas dropped toward them. When Blubb was in the bag and it was sealed shut, they picked it up and ran for the hedge. The ninjas swooped low to grab them.

Daphne, Harv, and Sidney didn't get far. The ninjas landed and encircled them. One ninja stepped forward and removed the black scarf from across his face. It was Lowell, of course.

"How nice to see you again, Sidney," Lowell said. "And I see you've brought Mr. Hero this time. Very thoughtful of you."

Sidney chuckled as if Lowell had said something humorous. "I'll warn you once," Sidney said, "Mr. Hero is more than you can handle. You wouldn't believe half of what he can do."

Lowell shook his head. "You heroes are all alike," he said. "Give me the bag!"

Daphne held her breath. This was the moment when everything could go wrong.

Sidney held out the bag. Just as they'd thought, Lowell pulled open the top and nodded in satisfaction. "One Perfect Artificial All-Purpose Champion of Truth and Justice," he said with a sneer. "Alias, the Purple Blob."

Just then Sidney grabbed back the bag, swung it around, and heaved it over the heads of the surrounding ninjas. It landed in the tangled bushes at the edge of Daphne's yard.

"Go get it," Lowell ordered the nearest ninjas. A bunch of them ran off. He glared at Sidney. "That was stupid," he said.

"Just like a hero," Sidney said and shrugged.

The ninjas returned a moment later with the plastic bag. Lowell took it and sniffed at the contents. "Not a pretty smell, is it?" he asked pleasantly.

"Being a hero is not always pretty work," Daphne said defiantly.

"My feeling exactly," Lowell said. "Consider yourselves lucky that Mr. Hero is all we wanted. Goodbye. Have a nice day." He wrapped the top of the bag around his fist. "Contact!" he cried.

Each ninja pulled a cord that hung from the side of his beanie, and the propeller racket started again. Lowell led his ninjas into the sky and then back the way they'd come.

"Did it work?" Daphne asked anxiously.

A ninja stepped from around the side of the house, and Daphne gasped.

"It worked," the ninja assured her. He flowed around till he became Blubb the kid again.

"Can I design a hero or what?" Sidney said.

"You did great," Daphne assured him. She beamed, feeling great.

Everything had gone exactly as planned. When Sidney threw Blubb into the bushes where the bag full of cat food was hidden, it gave Blubb a chance to crawl out and disguise himself as a ninja. Lowell hadn't actually counted the number of ninjas he sent to get the bag. If he had, the game would have been up because one extra ninja returned—Blubb.

"I sure hope Lowell likes cat food," Daphne said.

"Even if he does," Harv assured her, "he won't like Meowser brand."

Sidney laughed loudly. "Now that we know for sure that my aunt Millicent gives information to him, we can make sure that she hears all kinds of crazy stuff. It won't take long for Lowell to notice how unreliable she is and stop asking her for information." The thought seemed to please him.

Then Daphne caught a glimpse of her father walking up the driveway with his briefcase under his arm and his tie loosened.

"Blubb," she cried, "be a cat!"

Blubb became a vaguely purple cat who strolled out and sat at her feet.

Mr. Trusk noticed them and waved. "I see you've made some friends, Daf," he said.

"Right, Dad." She introduced Harv and Sidney. She was not too specific about who Sidney was. She didn't want to even *start* explaining that she and her friends had just postponed Lowell's enslavement of the Earth. It occurred to her that Blubb could have remained a kid. But it was too late for him to change back.

"What's this?" he asked, nodding at Blubb.

"One of Harv's cats," Daphne told him. "His name is Blubb, which is short for Robert."

Mr. Trusk stared at Blubb for a moment, and Daphne tried to remain calm. "Awfully big cat," was all he said. "So, what are you guys doing?"

"Just hacking around," Daphne assured him. "How was your date last night?"

Mr. Trusk shrugged. "She seemed very interested in using the right fork," he said.

"Too bad," Daphne said. Actually, she was relieved. Using the right fork had never been very important to her.

"She's not the only fish in the sea," Mr. Trusk said. He soon went into the house.

An idea struck Daphne that pleased her so much she could not keep from turning to Blubb with a sudden grin. "How would you like to be my brother?" she asked. He might be her only chance to have one. And though she'd known Blubb only a short time, the adventures they'd shared made her feel as if she'd known him for years.

"Can I be your brother and still be the Perfect Artificial All-Purpose Champion of Truth and Justice?"

"I would insist on it."

"All right, then. I'm your brother."

"But in front of my father you're a cat. Agreed?"

Blubb nodded.

"You're forgetting one thing," Sidney said.

Here it comes, Daphne thought sadly. Sidney was about to remind her that Blubb belonged to him.

Sidney wiggled a finger at Blubb. "You have to promise you'll come with me to school so I can get my final grade. You owe me that much."

Blubb nodded solemnly.

"That's it?" Daphne asked.

"That's it," Sidney said. He smiled shyly. "I figure I owe you something for saving me. And Mr. Hero, er, Blubb doesn't seem to mind."

"What about me?" Harv asked.

"We'll work something out," Sidney assured him. "Maybe a free pass for life to Uncle Alexander's Ice Cream."

"Maybe free classes at Paladin Tech," Harv countered.

Daphne wanted classes, too, but she didn't feel she could ask for them, considering she already got Blubb.

"Maybe," Sidney agreed.

Daphne was glad the telephone company had transferred her father, glad they'd moved to this town, to this neighborhood, into this house. In a place like this, Daphne decided, you never knew what was next. Her father might even find a wife. Daphne looked at Harv and Sidney and Blubb. They were all great guys, heroic guys, and not too conventional to be interesting. Anything could happen.

MEL GILDEN is the author of more than thirty middle-grade and young adult books, including *Star Trek®: Deep Space Nine™: The Pet*. He has written five novels for adults, including two Star Trek® books. In addition, Gilden is a radio personality, and has written and developed cartoons for television. He lives in Los Angeles, California, and still hopes to be an astronaut when he grows up.

DEBBY YOUNG is an illustrator and creative developer for children's television and advertising. Her work includes toys and merchandising, projects with Marvel Comics, and kids' books like *My Brother Blubb.* She currently resides in Manhattan.